# North from Amarillo

After eight long bloody years of drifting and warfare, Stretch McQuade came home. The ranch was run down: he had expected that but was willing to work to get it up and running again. What he didn't expect was to find his father crippled by a suspect 'accident' and tended to by a strange woman who seemed to have him under her control.

Old enemies were waiting to settle old scores, but the newest, most dangerous enemy of all was Yankee Reconstruction.

Someone had forgotten to tell *them* the war was supposed to be over.

# North from Amarillo

Jake Douglas

A Black Horse Western

ROBERT HALE · LONDON

© Jake Douglas 2007
First published in Great Britain 2007


ISBN 978-0-7090-8234-7


Robert Hale Limited
Clerkenwell House
Clerkenwell Green
London EC1R 0HT

Typeset by
Derek Doyle & Associates, Shaw Heath
Printed and bound in Great Britain by
Antony Rowe Limited, Wiltshire

# CHAPTER 1

# SOLDIER BOY

The image of the old ranch from eight long years ago was as near as dammit to the real thing. A mite more dilapidated, maybe, fences needing repair, plenty of weeds, although down one side there was a splash of colour – flowers? Hard to believe: the Old Man was never a gardener.

The barn doors were sagging at crazy angles, rocking slightly in the afternoon wind. Surprisingly, there were six or eight horses in the corrals; one stood out – a roan mare. The big corral needed uprights and some fresh lodgepole rails, but the smaller one, the one in use, seemed as if it had had some attention lately. Mmm, a little unexpected.

There was something different about the front steps leading to the porch where the Old Man had kept his cane chair that was no longer there. The angle didn't allow a proper view of the steps but they seemed to be tilted to one side – or collapsed, maybe.

But it was home, and home had been the main vision to hold on to during those just-past blood-soaked years.

I stood in the stirrups to get a better view, the trail-worn gelding under me grunting with the shift of my weight. No sign of riders – or the Old Man. Sun flashed from the front wall which told me that the glass was still surprisingly intact in the two windows, one either side of the door. The roof was in pretty good shape and a thin shimmer above the fieldstone chimney told me there had been a fire going recently. By now my heart was thudding in my chest.

It had been a long time since I'd seen the Old Man and we hadn't parted on good terms. . . .

'Don't look so bad.'

I eased down into the saddle and hipped to look at my three companions, pushing my battered campaign hat forward over my eyes. It was Toohey who had spoken, his grizzled face beard-shagged like the rest of us. Our clothes were dark with sweat, ragged and filthy from months of travel and sleeping in the open. We smelled sour, worse than any hogpen I could remember. *Johnny Rebs returning home – soldiers all.*

And we all had guns. I was lucky, I toted a Colt single-action percussion pistol in an officer's holster that I had cut the flap off. I'd also notched it a little so I could slip my finger through the trigger guard a mite more easily. My rifle was the prize, a Henry, one with the brass action plate and a barrel as long as a damn musket. That made it more accurate than most guns that were fed a diet of rimfire cartridges. The only other one with a rifle was young Denny.

He had a Spencer but it wasn't in very good shape. Morg carried a Gunnison and Griswald revolver, Toohey a heavy old Walker that pulled at his rope belt.

We looked what we were: a dangerous foursome on the drift, with eyes weary and bleary from killing that had eventually become nothing more than routine for us all.

Morg hawked and spat, wiping his beard absently, his one eye squinted against the sun. 'Gonna call out the Old Man before we ride in?'

'No wonder you lived so long,' I told him with a wry smile. 'Cautious Charley – but, yeah, I'll ride on down and check it out, signal if it's safe.' *Cautious? We had to be the way things had been – and still were, these days. . . .*

'What if it ain't safe?' asked young Denny. He always looked worried but I'd seen him once, laughing and dancing while Yankee cannon balls shattered the adobe walls of the farmhouse we were sheltering in. But he'd been a mite slow since being caught in a shell blast while crossing the river at Madison's Ferry.

'You'll know if it ain't safe, Denny,' said Toohey, grizzled and at least seven years older then the forty he admitted to. 'Stretch won't come back to tell you anythin'.'

Denny immediately assumed his worried look, hunched and pale. I said brightly enough, 'Find some cover, but where you can still see the yard, Den.'

I left them to it, riding on down slowly, easing the

Henry in the grass-rope loop I used to sling it from the pommel.

I was surprised at how tight my chest felt, how my heartbeat had quickened, as I rode towards the silent, sprawling house I'd left as a boy and was now returning to as a man. *Just what kind of man only time would tell. . . .*

The door opening suddenly startled me and I tugged the reins, but immediately dug in my heels again, bringing a shake of the head and a rough snort from the gelding: *make up your mind*, he was telling me.

The next surprise was the sight of the Old Man. He was in a wheelchair and I could see now why the porch steps had looked so queer: they had been replaced by a short wooden ramp.

And then came the third shock, clipping me like an uppercut from my first drill sergeant.

My father's wheelchair was being pushed by a woman. From what I could make out, she was in her early thirties, not very tall, perhaps carrying a little more weight than she needed. But she had raven-black hair piled up on top of her head and I glimpsed a pale oval of face, with cool, appraising eyes taking in every aspect of me as I reined up the gelding a few feet from the porch.

I tried to keep my voice steady. 'Howdy, Pa. Got the place looking OK. Not prime, but OK.'

He was thinner, like his grey hair, face gaunt, cheeks hollow, eyes set way back in their sockets, but still with that glint you only get when light strikes steel in a certain way. 'You took your time gettin' here.' His voice was wheezy and much weaker. *What the hell had happened to him? And who the hell was she?*

'Country's in turmoil, almost as bad as when the guns were still firing. Not easy to travel a couple of thousand miles when it's like that, Pa.'

'You been gone over eight years!'

'Long, hard years, Pa. A war on during most of 'em.'

He grunted. 'Well, you're here now, God knows why. Who's that ragtag bunch hidin' behind the barn?'

I was watching the woman as I spoke. Her eyes had never left me since she'd appeared on the porch. Nor did they even when she reached down and adjusted the checked rug over my father's legs, which looked thin and bony beneath the wool.

'Some friends of mine. Thought the ranch might need some attention. And they're looking for work.'

'The ranch will get whatever attention it needs, Dean,' the woman said to me in a cool voice, letting me know she had been with my father long enough for him to have told her about me.

'They call me "Stretch" now, ma'am. Seems I've growed some since leaving here.'

'Your name's Dean!' Pa growled, wheezing again.

It had been my mother's maiden name and I knew that was why he sounded riled at my use of the nick- name.

'Sure, Pa, I use it when I need to. But to most folk I'm just Stretch McQuade.'

'It's certainly an apt enough title,' the woman said with the hint of a smile. 'I'm Eleanor Chapman. My friends call me Ellie, mostly.'

'That *Mrs* Chapman?' I'd noticed a slim band of gold on her third finger, left hand. I guess I clipped the words more than I meant to, for her eyes flashed some and the Old Man stirred, tried to get enough breath to put me in my place.

Her hand squeezed his shoulder, calming him. Her gaze was direct. 'Yes, Mrs Chapman. My husband was killed at Secand Manassis.'

'That's what the Yankees call Bull Run. . . .'

'You hadn't noticed by my speech that I'm a Northerner?' There was a hint of amusement in her tone and a slight stretching of those full red lips.

'I had a hunch,' I admitted, though I hadn't really picked her accent because she'd said so little. 'You something to do with the Reconstruction?'

'By Godfrey, boy, you're a damn sight more sassy than I recall! I'd take the switch to you if you'd spoken so disrespectfully to a guest before you run out on me.'

'Long time ago, Pa. I don't think I'd stand still for a switchin' now.'

His face darkened and those old eyes – were they more cloudy, opaque, than I recalled? – bored hard into me.

'Ellie has been nursin' me and takin' care of me,' he said hoarsely. 'Show her some respect!'

I didn't look at her, kept focused on him. 'What happened?' I gestured to his wheelchair.

'Half-broke horse. Damn wrangler I had was no good. Hadn't had time to train him the way I did you. Tried to shoot him after I come home from hospital but the sonuver ran and I only winged him. He was eatin' like a horse for some time though – standin' up.'

I smiled. This was more like the old Pa. But it was no smiling matter, being stuck in a wheelchair. 'You ever be able to walk?' The McQuades were always direct.

'It's possible,' the woman answered for him. 'But not very likely, I'm afraid.'

Irritably, he waved a hand to change the subject.

'How old you be now?' he growled, chest heaving with his noisy breathing. 'Twenty-four, twenty-five. . . ?'

'Somewhere in there.'

'At that age I was sweatin' my guts out, brush-poppin' mavericks, ridin' down to Mexico, tradin' lead with *bandidos* who'd cut your manhood off and stuff it in your mouth! 'Scuse me, Ellie, but it's true—'

'Now don't get all worked-up, Hiram,' she said soothingly, throwing me a narrow-eyed look. 'You're upsetting your father, Dean.'

'He's upsetting himself. He's riled at me and wants to make sure I know it. I'd like to think I know him a mite better than you do.'

'That's enough!' snapped the Old Man. 'You can't be civil, take your ragtags and get off this ranch!'

I was ready to do it, but stubbornness stopped me. 'Pa, it's over eight years since I left, and I spent six of 'em dodging Yankee bullets. I survived, and all that time I wanted nothing better than to return home and make sure you were all right. . . .' I paused.

'You needn't've damn well bothered yourself!'

11

I sighed. 'I guess you're being looked after well enough, so if you'll let us overnight in the barn, we'll be moving along come sun-up.'

He chewed one end of his long frontier moustache. He didn't answer and she leaned over him and spoke quietly so I didn't hear her words.

He kind of snorted as she straightened and then he looked at me without warmth or welcome.'One night – in the barn. We got no vittles to spare. You want meat, you go hunt it – an' don't you shoot none of my beeves or I'll have the law on you!'

*Law?* What did he mean? Yankee Reconstructionists? Didn't matter. Mean old coot was just being as cantankerous as he could. *He hadn't changed! But I had. . . .*

I wheeled the gelding and rode back to where the others were waiting, told them.

Morg scratched at the black leather of his eyepatch, always a sign of irritation, but remained silent. Denny looked puzzled. Toohey pursed his lips.

'Welcome home, soldier-boy,' he said quietly.

# CHAPTER 2

# FLAG

We didn't have much tobacco between us but I took enough to roll a slim cigarette, crawled out of my bedroll spread on a layer of musty straw and went to the door of the barn. I lit up, leaning a shoulder against one creaking, sagging door and drew the smoke deep into my lungs.

It was half-moon bright, plenty of shadows, light patches strung like shallow pools in a mid-summer creek.

I couldn't sleep, although the others were snoring and tossing about. I *should've* been able to sleep: we'd had one helluva journey down here to the Caprock escarpment fringing the Staked Plains – *Llano Estacado* as most Texans called them or just plain 'Llano', the old hands using the Spanish pronunciation – 'Yarno'.

I hadn't expected a fatted calf and a welcoming handshake, but I admitted to a hurt at the way my

13

homecoming had turned out. *That damn woman had made it go all wrong!*

I knew straight away I wasn't being quite fair: sure, it would've been better if I had met the Old Man alone and we might've talked out our differences, and she hadn't really interfered. Though she had said enough to let me know that she had the Old Man's ear. But who was she? What did she want here? Nurse, he'd said, but what was there for her to do now except push him around in his chair?

*There was Flag, of course!*

Flag – that was what we called the ranch. It was our brand, an easy one to burn into the hide of the long-horn cattle we ran. *Or did we? I hadn't seen much sign of cattle on the way in, only a handful. Hell! Maybe the Reconstruction had already taken them! I'd find out come morning.*

No, I wouldn't. He wanted me off the place by sun-up. I'd been riled enough to tell him I'd be gone by then, but I didn't really want to go. Morgan and Denny and Toohey were all homeless men. Families swallowed by the monster that had ravaged the land these past six years. No homes to go to; no kin to look up. That was when I realized how important family was. My only living kin was the Old Man. So I'd put it to the others:

'How'd you like to ride back to Texas with me? Live and work on our ranch in the Panhandle, not far from Amarillo?'

None of them had let their eagerness show. But I'd seen it all the same. 'Long way, Stretch,' Morg said, with his usual wariness.

'So? You got somewhere else you want to be?'

Of course none of them had. We started out from way up in Illinois where news of Appomattox had reached us, and if we thought the war was ended we soon found out different.

Yankees were everywhere and they aimed to ram down the throat of every Reb they came across that they had won the goddamn war – and don't you forget it! If you were wearing anything grey that looked like it might be part of a Confederate uniform, you'd better not expect a brotherly handshake from anyone in Union blue. All we had were grey rags, the remnants of our uniforms. So our passage south was not without incident and excitement of a kind we could do without.

We did some hard riding and honed the talents we'd picked up during the fighting: how to steal grub and clothing and ammunition, even weapons. We were caught – or Toohey and Denny were – in one town that was overflowing with a Yankee garrison. The boys were beat-up and ready for lynching when Morg and me found a case of dynamite in an abandoned mine tunnel.

'Christ! It's oozin'!' Morg said, backing off, eyes bulging at sight of the glittering amber beads sweating out of the old sticks in the rotting paper. 'Breathe heavy and that stuff'll go up and we'll be waitin' at Hell's gate before Denny and Toohey get there!'

'Well, we don't have detonators,' I pointed out. 'So this being kind of sensitive might be all for the good.'

'You're crazy! You can't handle this stuff! Try to pick up a stick and you'll lose an arm!'

15

I knew his caution was from experience but I'd done a lot of crazy things and taken mad risks during the fighting. So I eased a few sticks out while Morg hunkered down behind a boulder. I tied them with grass strips, made a paper tube and filled it with blackpowder from my flask and pushed in three or four percussion caps that I couldn't really spare, thumbing the lot into the middle of the bundle.

'It won't work! You'll kill us both!'

Morg had come out from behind his boulder. 'You best ride on, Morg, but I aim to blast the boys out of that jail.'

Leery or not, Morg was no coward and he didn't let his friends down. We managed to plant the bomb under the barred window of the cell where Denny and Toohey were, called hoarsely to them to take cover using their bunks and mattresses. It was just after sundown when I lay prone on the high rock just outside the town, the jail being on the outskirts.

The Henry rifle which I'd taken from a Yankee lieutanant I'd killed at a place called Hat Creek, had a graduated sight and I took careful aim at the brass base of the rimfire cartridge I'd added to my paper tube and percussion caps as it glowed in the dusk.

I knew the Henry was accurate as long as a man could take his time and I took my time, had Morg practically dancing a jig before I was satisfied with the bead and squeezed the trigger. I never did hear the crack of the rifle: the explosion came too fast, drowned it – and nearly killed us with flying chunks of adobe and a couple of clattering, ringing iron bars bouncing off our rock.

It was touch and go getting away but I'd left a second bundle of dynamite beside the trail where it went through a narrow pass only a few yards long but it cut through a barrier range. It took three shots from my Colt before I hit the right spot and then I heard a hundred bells ringing in my head, was stung by gravel that raked me like a load of buckshot and half fell from the saddle.

But we fazed those Yankees and were long gone before they found a way over the range.

South. That was the way we wanted to go.

But we couldn't do it in a straight line and had to head in every direction of the compass – including back north at one stage – to clear the blue-bellies who were everywhere now.

We had growling, empty bellies for days on end and twice on deserts Toohey knew about we near died of thirst. Somehow we not only got ourselves across but our suffering mounts, too.

And when we cleared the last one, we ran into a Yankee patrol who wanted some sport with us and drove us back into the desert, setting us up as targets for their men lining the rocks. We fooled the sons of bitches by each taking a tumble and when they came to gloat, we jumped up and shot three of them before they knew what had happened.

We reciprocated their kindness to us by driving the survivors out into the desert – afoot. With one canteen of water between the eight of them.

With fresh mounts and rough though adequate food for at least a week, now, we moved on into Indian country.

And that almost did for us.

We'd crossed Kansas by that time and still had the strip of Indian Territory to ride through before we reached the high plains of northern Texas. It was the stamping ground of Kiowa and Commanche and Apache.

I think it was Kiowa who hit us as we passed a black mesa one afternoon. They came from out of the deep shadow, maybe ten or a dozen, whooping like they were trying to let their ancestors know they were still up to putting a few half-starved palefaces under the sod. And the whoops were interspersed with gunshots.

'God-damn!' Toohey exclaimed: he was our chief blasphemer. 'Them lousy Yankees leave their guns *everywhere*! Don't they know them red devils will sell their heathen souls – if you can say it that way! – just to hold a white-man's gun and shoot it?'

No one answered: we were too busy thundering along the trail. Our mounts were near-jaded by now and we'd been hungry for two days and there was less than a cupful of water between us in our canteens. We were not in very good shape to fend off a bunch of white-hating Indians.

But there was no choice and we found a small saucer-like depression – buffalo wallow, I guess – and we tried to cover the four major points of the compass. We needed to watch our ammunition. Powder was low and there hadn't been any .44/.40 calibre rimfire cartridges with that Yankee patrol we'd ousted. The Indians were shooting like they had access to an arsenal. But they were lousy shots and I could tell by the sound that some of the guns were old trade rifles, likely with barrels bound up by wire.

But I heard the lash of a Springfield and the dull thudding of a Spencer carbine, too. I sighted and followed the racing path of a redskin lying along the back of a stretched-out pony with yellow and black symbols painted on its sweating hide. He was shooting a lever action of some sort and I let him have a slug as he half-lifted – I suspect that a cartridge had jammed in the ejector port and he didn't know how to clear it. Not that it mattered. My bullet knocked him clear off his mount and I quickly found another target right behind the man I'd downed.

This one was so carried away with his blood lust that he was actually standing on the back of his horse, like a circus performer, trying to push a shell into the breech of his stubby rifle.

I wasn't the only one who thought he made a great target: Toohey and Denny both fired almost simultaneously with me. The red devil was flung and kicked around in mid-air by the lead as if he was dangling at the end of a string. Then he dropped and two of his companions rode right over him. A bad day for him. . . .

Then it was our turn. Another eight or ten Indians came thundering out of the mesa's shadow and although there was a storm of arrows, indicating they had more bows than guns, I knew we were in trouble. For one thing, two of our mounts went down like pin cushions and Toohey had to cut their throats to put them out of their misery and save us from being brained by their thrashing hoofs.

Morg's gun was giving him trouble. Denny was shooting well but was almost out of ammunition. Toohey,was as calm as ever, moving at a normal pace from position to position, firing once from each place. I don't know if he hit his targets but I'd guess not, judging by the number of Indians who came sweeping in on a death charge.

'Might not get to see that ranch of yours after all, Stretch,' Morgan said, in his usual cheerful way.

Then it was gunsmoke and noise and sleek, copper-coloured bodies hurtling through the air, blades with buckskin-wrapped handles slashing and seeking white-man's blood. The stench of unwashed bodies – likely ours were as unpalatable to them as theirs were to us – as we clashed hand-to-hand. I brained one brave with the curved brass butt of the Henry and then it was knocked from my hands and a tomahawk blade whistled past my face, almost taking my nose with it. The Kiowa stumbled and I gave him a boot under his breechclout that didn't do him a lot of good. My hands were empty so I raked backward with my spurs and he screamed as his face opened up and then his chest.

I was felled by a blow from behind, sprawled on hands and knees, shook my head to clear my vision and had a hazy impression of a stone-headed lance coming straight at my chest. I feebly tried to beat it to one side and through the hell and cacophony in my head I heard a long thudding of gunfire and the lance-wielding Indian was jerking and stumbling with blood oozing from at least five bullet holes in his upper body.

I had no time to see what had happened as another one, already wounded, stumbled towards me with his knife. I felt the blade leave a burning line across my belly and then I had his forearm in a grip, lifted a leg and broke his arm across my knee. He screamed and started to collapse but I grabbed the knife and buried it to the hilt in his throat.

Hot blood washed over my hands and I stepped back: I hate knife-fighting, can't abide the slicing of cold steel through warm flesh . . . unless it's saving my life.

I became aware of shouting – in American – and the odd crack of a pistol, the drumming of horses' hoofs and was suddenly surrounded by men in blue uniforms. *Damn! The Yankees have overrun us . . .* Then my senses came out of their spin and I realized this was a Yankee patrol and they'd saved our bacon.

They were in charge of a Lieutenant Adam Clegg, and they had been on the far side of the mesa on the lookout for rumoured renegade Indians. Hearing the gunfire, they came a-thundering.

'First Yankee I've been happy to see,' I told Clegg as we shook hands. 'McQuade, Stretch McQuade.'

He was a man in his late twenties and had the look of one who had breathed much gunsmoke these last few years.

'Making your way home, Reb?' There was no twisting insult in the term, just a genuine query.

'Father's got a ranch in the Panhandle.'

'Come far?'

'Springfield,' and he arched his eyebrows so I told him of our adventures – some, anyway: I somehow forgot about tangling with those butt-headed Yanks in the desert.

'You've had it rough. All six years of the war, eh? Must've been but a kid when you joined.'

'Sixteen or thereabouts.'

He nodded. 'About the same age as my brother – stupid kid. Wanted to be like me – big brother! Lost him at The Wilderness.'

'I missed that one, thank God.'

He had a square jaw and a thick black moustache. He scratched at his chin. 'Reb, we've all had it rough. One of your sawbones tried to save my kid brother but it wasn't to be. So, I guess it's time we all calmed down; we'll escort you through the Territory and see you on your way home. I'm luckier than some. I've a big mansion to go back to up in Virginia, but I don't seem to be in any hurry to make the move. Maybe that Reb ball that grazed my head addled my brains!'

He was as good as his word and gave us grub and some ammo before leaving us to continue on home. *What I thought was home, anyway. . . .*

I finished the cigarette and crushed it out against the weathered barn door before dropping it to the ground. The stars were blazing now the moon was setting and there was a deep shadow cast over the front of the ranch house. I stared at the place, wondering what the Old Man was doing. Was he sleeping? Dreaming? Thinking about me. . . ? The old days, when Ma was alive and Willard, the older brother who had died in a gunfight in Amarillo before the war broke. I tried not to think about Willard, a good brother, and I missed him. . . .

It was after that that Pa began treating me harshly and I finally upped and left. His parting words were,

'I ever see you round here again, I'll shoot you like the ungrateful wretch you are! Now git and to hell with you!'

'Wonder why I ever had the notion I'd be welcomed back here?' I murmured aloud. But the pull of the place had been strong, especially so after surviving some raid or bombardment or bloody battle. *Home* was how I thought of it.

Flag seemed like the place I wanted to be . . . *needed* to be?

I stiffened suddenly. There was movement on the front porch in the deep shadow. A match flared and touched to the end of a cigarillo and for a moment I thought it was the Old Man and even started forward a step, ready to talk.

But then I saw the features in the flare.

It was Eleanor Chapman.

# CHAPTER 3

# WRANGLER

She watched me cross the yard, drew deeply on the cigarillo, exhaled through her nostrils.

'I wondered if you could sleep.' When I didn't say anything, she added, 'I knew you'd be upset by Hiram's attitude.'

'I guess I expected it. Still not easy to swallow.'

'His bark's worse than his bite. He doesn't really want you to go away again.'

'Not the message I got.'

'No. He's quick-tempered, says things he doesn't mean – but I thought you'd know all that. . . ?'

'I was just a kid when he started beating me and treating me like dirt. It was what he did that drove me away, not why. I couldn't figure out the reasons. Something to do with Willard. But over the years it stopped bothering me.'

'Now it's reared its ugly head again?'

I shrugged. 'Maybe I'll handle it better now.'

Her teeth flashed briefly.'Like lying awake worrying about him?'

I was getting tired of this, making me the stranger. 'I've had to worry about a lot of things the past eight years – a new one for me is you.'

She seemed genuinely startled. 'Me?'

'Who are you? What d'you want here?'

'Well, you've inherited your father's directness!'

I waited.

'When he was hurt in that horse fall—'

'When did that happen by the way?'

'Six months ago, just after the war ended. He gave a couple of townsmen work. One was Skip someone or other and he claimed to be a good wrangler, but he didn't break-in the horses properly, it seems.'

'Skip Dexter?'

'I don't know his other name.'

Pa surely would have had more sense than to hire a strutting no-good like Skip Dexter! But then, ranch hands would've been mighty scarce until those who went to the war began to drift home, and the ranch needed a lot of attention. 'How bad are his injuries?'

'His legs mostly. Old bones not knitting well. Possibility of some spinal damage which may prevent him from ever walking again.'

*Jesus!*

'I was assisting in the infirmary and we . . . well, we seemed to get along very well. And your father asked me to come and live out here and take care of him until either he could walk again, or, if he was unable to, to be his companion and nurse combined.'

'How's he paying you?'

The cigarillo glowed, smoke drifted across the porch. 'I believe that's something that should remain just between Hiram and me.'

'Not if the ranch is involved.' I didn't want to get into this, legacies and entitlement and so on, but she annoyed me, the way she was so superior, trying to make me feel an outsider because I'd been absent for so long. True, I didn't know the state of Flag or anything else to do with it: I didn't even know anything about *him*, whether he'd changed or not, but I had a *right* to know, whether thc Old Man was going to cut me in or out. I hadn't come back to claim the ranch: I'd come back to see him, and while I was hurting some because of his treatment, I wasn't totally surprised.

I hadn't exactly been Mr Sweetness-and-Light, either.

The big surprise was this woman, moving into the house, even into his bedroom for all I knew or cared. No! I cared, all right. . . .

'You might figure it's your business only, Mrs Chapman, but I grew up here and whatever happened in the past is not a bother to me now. But your being here affects things and I'm not yet sure just how.'

I had the impression that she smiled again, although I couldn't see her face clearly. 'You're afraid he might leave the ranch to me if anything happens to him.'

'More that because he might leave Flag to you, something *could* happen to him.'

It brought her to her feet and she had a right to be

26

riled. She flicked the burning cigarillo at my face but I moved my head slightly and it shot over my shoulder to burst in a shower of sparks on the ramp.

'How dare you! You damned arrogant streak of misery!' She hissed the words and sounded just like a rattler before it strikes. 'You ride in here like a dirty saddletramp, insult your father, get him, a sick man, all hot and bothered, then – then you insult *me*! Someone who truly cares for him, is trying to help and comfort him through what is really a very difficult time!'

If she hadn't given herself such a good pat on the back, I might have felt bad about what I'd said and backed down. But it seemed to me she was *trying* to give herself a good image, hammering at it, so maybe she was trying just a little too hard. I'd have respected her more if she hadn't stressed what a good-intentioned, caring person she was. Or wanted folk to think she was. . . .

I'd kicked around the trails and hell towns a deal before the war started, and I had met older, more experienced men, and thank God I did, because a couple of them got me out of trouble I walked into blindly because of my inexperience and ignorance. It had made me leery of folk who beat their own drum when there was really no need for it.

'Well, that's it, Mrs Chapman. Out in the open. I don't aim to stand by and see anyone sweet talk my father into parting with something he's worked for all his life.'

'Especially if it's something you want yourself!' She was breathing hard now, air hissing through her nostrils. 'You just wait until Hank gets here! He'll soon straighten you out!'

She turned abruptly towards the door as I asked, 'Who's Hank?'

Hand on the latch she half-turned, and this time I saw the crooked smile. 'You'll find out.'

She went inside, closing the door quietly.

Morgan's one eye followed me as we cooked a meagre breakfast, a handful of oatmeal, corn and wheat-grain rolled in flour and cooking grease. It put a lining in your stomach even if it didn't do much else. Denny was trying to get his spiky blond hair to stay down while Toohey was cleaning the big Walker.

Morgan said, 'Sleep well?'

I just looked at him.

'Thought I heard someone movin' around in the dark.'

I still said nothing, flipped a couple of the wheat-cakes. He sighed. 'Where we goin'?'

'Haven't decided.'

'Has to be up to you – none of us know Texas.' It was his way of telling me the others would do whatever I wanted. I unbent a little, feeling bad about my grumpiness.

'Fact is, might have a word with the Old Man. Place needs fixing-up, and now. I guess the Yankees give him a hard time like they give everyone else we spoke to who're caught up in Reconstruction – won't be too many hands he can hire hereabouts. Not ones who know ranch work, anyway.'

Morgan's single eye glittered briefly. 'Family ties

givin' you a nudge.' It wasn't a question.'Nothin' wrong with that. But your Old Man turns out to be hard as he seems and him an' me're gonna go head to head.'

'You'll have to stand in line. I was talking with the woman last night.' I ignored the sharpening of Morg's face and the way one eyebrow arched. Both Denny and Toohey looked my way, too. 'Seems Pa hired one of the local fellers to wrangle the horses but he picked a wrong'un. Skip Dexter; someone he should've known was a lousy bet—'

'Mebbe he had someone urgin' him?' Toohey grated.

'Occurred to me, too. Like to know who and why. 'Cause Skip Dexter was the one responsible for not breaking-in that mount that crippled the Old Man.'

No one said anything right then and I'd slid the unappetizing wheatcakes on to the platters when Toohey spoke up, 'Learn anythin' about the woman?'

I nodded, let them wait a little while I tried some of the mess on my plate. Surprisingly it wasn't too bad, chewy and crunchy both, hot, but flavoured some by the old well-used cooking grease. 'Not a lot. Enough to make me worry about how much of a hold she has over the Old Man.'

Toohey grunted. Denny just stared: it was always hard to know what he was thinking. Morgan whistled softly, tunelessly, withholding comment. But the whistle gave him away: he used it often when he didn't want to upset any of us by making a remark we mightn't care for.

'When you goin' to see the Old Feller?' he asked eventually as we finished eating, and went to the well to wash the stuff down, the cool water as sweet as I remembered.

I had the ladle and drained it, saw Pa come out on to the porch, pushed along by the Chapman woman. 'Might's well make it now.'

Denny took the ladle and dipped it into the wooden pail sitting on the fieldstone rim of the well as I walked up towards the house, wiping the back of a hand across my wet mouth.

'Nice morning,' I ventured.

The woman inclined her head, face expression-less. The Old Man filled his pipe and she scraped a vesta into flame, held it for him while he puffed clouds of aromatic smoke. She leaned down and said something. He glanced up sourly. 'You got over your colic or whatever was makin' you sour-guts last night?'

'I feel all right,' I answered neutrally. 'How about you?' *Never give an inch: he'd taught me that.*

He grunted, puffed. The woman busied herself with trivial things, adjusting the blanket and setting the wheels firmly and so on, anything that would keep her from looking at me. But I think she was speaking softly to him. *Giving him orders?*

'It's past sun-up,' Pa said suddenly.

I felt a knot in the belly. 'Must've slept in. We'll be on our way pretty soon. Just . . . just wanted to make sure you don't need anything doing about the place before we pull out.' I gestured vaguely to where the others waited by the well. 'Mightn't look much but between the four of us, we could knock this place into shape pretty damn quick – if you wanted us to.'

He thought about it. The woman wasn't doing anything now, but she was watching me. I think she nudged his shoulder. 'Can't pay you. Feed you and give you a place to sleep. No more.'

'S'pose that'll be all right.' I hope it sounded grudging: didn't want him to think I was giving in too easily. 'I'll go ask the boys. . . .'

I saw the woman nudge him this time and then Pa took the pipe from his leathery old lips and said, kind of snarling, 'Aaah, quit this! You can see blamed well the place is fallin' apart! It's your duty to help get it back into shape. If you need help then I guess them three'll be OK. Leastwise, they're Southerners, ain't they?'

'You got Georgia, Alabama and Tennessee represented there.'

'Good enough. You can start on the barn and corrals. Later, we'll need more hosses for a remuda.'

I gave him a sharp look. 'I didn't see any cows.'

His mouth twisted in what I guessed was a smile: he wasn't a man I remembered as ever having smiled much. 'Yankees have a head tax on Texas beef, so they don't see 'em, neither! But they're hereabouts. One of Ellie's Yankee visitors happened to mention that a castrated male is worth about four bucks here, but little ways north they'll pay forty dollars for the same scrawny steer. Seems someone gave 'em a taste for Texas beef.'

'We heard the Army needs meat supplied to their men to the west of here, too,' Ellie Chapman said, trying to sound as if she was a part of this.

Bad-manneredly, I ignored her. But I wondered about her 'Yankee friend', as Pa put it, visiting here. Was his name Hank? 'OK, we'll get started. We'll need some nails and wire and such, tools . . . you got 'em?'

'Have to go to town. I'm cleaned out. Byron at the General Store'll give us credit. I'll write him a note.'

I liked that 'us'.

And I liked the idea of going into Amarillo – I knew the places Skip Dexter used to hang out. And I wanted a few words with that son of a bitch.

Quincey Byron had been a handsome man in his day. His features were still OK, even and pleasant, but he had lost a deal of hair and what remained, tufted above his ears and around the back of his skull, was white, although he wasn't as old as the Old Man.

He made no bones about giving Pa credit, made up the order. Denny was outside stowing it in the old buckboard we'd found in the barn and greased-up before bringing it to town. Toohey was prowling as he always did, alone, looking into parts of town most men wouldn't bother with. Morg was across at the livery, trying to sell a Yankee jack-knife he had, stamped 'US Cavalry', so he could buy some new trousers – his were even more ragged than mine.

Through the store window, I saw Denny whistling to himself as he stacked the kegs of nails and bales of wire, and, beyond him the townsfolk. There were a lot of blue uniforms out there and the Yankee soldiers seemed to think any woman was fair game. I saw several arguments.

'You don't even remember me, do you, Dean?'

I swung around and on the other side of the counter was a girl: blonde, fair-skinned, green eyes like a shadowed mountain pool, dressed in grey gingham, flour showing on her hands and forearms as she closed off a heavy brown-paper bag.

'By Godfrey – not Kitty? Not little Kitty Byron. . . ?'

She smiled. 'Not so little now.' She sure wasn't!

'Me, neither.' I grinned, and gestured to her hair which was piled up on top of her head, sort of drawn across the back and held in place by a comb. 'No pigtails now for me to dip in the school inkwells.'

'I'll get you for that some day,' she smiled back. 'I warned you at school and I haven't forgotten. I'm sure that must be one reason you ran away all those years back.'

'Well – yeah, you had me scared, all right. If I'd known that freckled, funny-faced, sassy little kid was gonna turn out like this, though, I might not've run.'

Her smile was a trifle smaller now. 'You would've. You were the most stubborn boy I ever knew.'

'Maybe I've improved. Really good to see you again, Kit.'

'You, too, Dean.'

'They tend to call me Stretch now.'

She nodded. 'I wonder why – you sure have shot up.' She looked at my clothes. 'If you want some help choosing new trousers and shirt. . . ?'

I shook my head. 'Can't afford 'em. Pa only asked for credit on tools and such.'

'Dad?' Byron stood up from where he had been

33

filling a can with molasses from a keg on a low stand. 'Dean is in sore need of some new clothes – couldn't we extend credit. . . ?'

Byron pursed his lips. 'I know Hiram McQuade is good for it, but he didn't mention it in his note. If I thought he would approve—'

'Of course he will,' Kitty broke in. 'I mean, he wouldn't want his own son to get around in rags like that!'

I had nothing to say about that and finally Quincey nodded. 'Don't see why not. . . .'

'Mr Byron, I have three friends who've been with me for some years now. They'll be working the ranch with me. Could you. . . ?'

Byron sighed. 'Dean, I'll have to do it this way: I'll outfit your friends, but they'll have to pay me at least something when they draw their first wages.'

I said sure, not knowing if Pa had meant it when he said we'd have to work only for grub and beds.

'Oh!' Kitty made the exclamation suddenly, a hand going to her firm red mouth. 'That darn Skip Dexter! He – he seems to be picking on your friend in the buckboard. . . .'

I was already on the way to the street door, not really conscious of my hands fisting-up down at my sides.

# CHAPTER 4

# YANKEE TOWN

Dexter had changed plenty. He'd been a rawboned, jut-jawed bully with buck teeth and an arrogance that had buffaloed a lot of folk in town, even some adults, when hc was just a kid. Even then folk had seen something dangerous in him, something not quite sane.

We'd tangled of course, many times: Skip Dexter tangled with every kid in town, even the schoolteacher who was quite a size but ended up being scared of Skip. Of course, in those days there had been a couple more Dexters: the old man, always boozed-up and spoiling for a fight, and Dexter's big brother, Bruiser, a name well earned, and the idiot was proud of it.

But his father had been run over by a wagon one night before I quit Flag and I heard that Bruiser had been blown apart by a Yankee cannon ball at the battle at Monroe Station. But Skip seemed to have the same obnoxious, bullying swagger and he was using it on Denny, who was more puzzled than scared. The kid was a little too slow in his thinking since that shell blast to be scared right off. He might have even thought

Skip was just fooling about boisterously, but I could see he didn't like being man-handled by Dexter.

I walked right up, knocked Skip's hat off, twisted fingers in his hair and yanked hard. He yelled, releasing Denny, stumbled out of the buckboard on to the loading platform. He had put on a deal of weight and was a beefy, tough-looking man now, almost 200 pounds of him. Thick lips peeled back in a snarl, and for a moment he didn't recognize me as he straightened slowly. Then:

'Well, I'll be. . . ! That scarecrow surely ain't the smart-mouthed McQuade kid whose ass I used to kick!'

'Your big brother did the kicking, Skip, you only waded in after he'd softened me up.'

Dexter wiped the back of a meaty hand across damp nostrils, rubbed it on his shirt, the tails of which hung out of his belt on one side. His scary eyes narrowed. He spat. I don't know whether he aimed at my boots or not, but he missed. Just. Folk were beginning to gather. Denny watched, slack-jawed. Out of a corner of my eye, I saw Kitty and her father peering through the store window.

'So you come back, McQuade. Too bad. This weren't a bad town up till now. Maybe you should leave before you get settled in, huh? I mean, your old man ain't up to helpin' you and he's a stubborn ol' coot. Dare say he won't welcome you.'

'That's why I'm picking up things for him at the store, Skip. Because of you, he can't do chores himself now. I'll be working Flag for him.'

Dexter frowned. 'We-ell, I guess you might's well

36

leave again anyways.'

'No. I don't know how come Pa hired an incompetent like you to break his horses, but there's some settling to do between you and me: he might never walk again.'

'Aw, geez, ain't that a cryin' shame! Now if his saddle had slipped a little more he wouldn't have to worry about that – he'd be dead and helpin' the weeds grow in Boot Hill.'

That was it. Maybe he was trying to rile me enough to take first swing, but I read plenty into what he was saying: he'd fixed Pa's saddle when he'd been riding that horse that rolled on his legs, crushing them so badly. *But it sounded to me like it had been meant to kill him. Why?*

I was hot-tempered enough to step forward and swing and, of course, he was ready, although he didn't seem to be. He stepped aside nimbly enough for a man his size – he must've out-weighed me by nearly forty pounds – and moved to let my impetus carry me just past him. So he could reach my kidneys with one of those meaty fists.

I felt it, felt it like a mustang's kick slamming into me, and I went down on one knee. The crowd was vocal by now, but I couldn't make out any words because of the sudden roaring in my ears that threatened to explode my head. Skip was grinning – I saw that through cheesecloth, too, flecked with whirling bright lights – then his knee lifted towards my face. I had enough left to turn my head and it caught me alongside the jaw. I rolled back off the loading dock that was only a foot or so above the buckboard, sprawled amongst the kegs of nails and tools in the wagon's tray. Something mighty hard and made of iron scraped down my ribs and took what little breath I had left. The pain surged through me like fire. The buckboard creaked and rocked as Skip Dexter jumped into it. The two-horse team snorted and Denny yelled something, scrambling on to the dock.

Through a red haze, I saw Skip pick up the lean kid – he couldn't have weighed more then seventy, eighty pounds then – and throw him into the street. I glimpsed Denny rolling in the dust and a couple of townsmen helped him up, but by then I was moving over the gear in the buckboard, looking to murder Dexter.

Skip was grinning, enjoying this. He crouched, big hands ready, eyes bright with excitement and a good feeling because he was hurting someone – *me!* – and he let me go to him. I knew it was a mistake but I took a chance. I've always had good balance and I jumped to the narrow top of the keg of ten-penny nails, managed to stay put on one leg and swung my other boot into Skip's thick neck. It was really hardly any neck at all, just rigid muscle, wider than his head where his shoulders began to slope down.

But it hurt him and he grabbed at it, swaying. I jumped from the keg top, wrapped my arms about him and carried him over to the edge of the buck-board. Locked together, we rolled off into the street, under the stomping hoofs of the startled team as they began to prance.

We separated mutually and scrambled out to safety, getting to our feet at about the same time. I might have shaded him a mite, because I was moving in on him before he was properly upright. He still parried my first blow but he wasn't set to retaliate and my second hooked him under the jaw. His teeth clacked together and blood flowed from his split lip. I mashed it back against his teeth again with another straight right. His head jerked and he stepped back, unwillingly, but he retreated just the same – and just a little faster than I allowed so that my next punch whistled past his face.

Dexter ducked under and came up inside my arm, ramming upwards with his bullet head. I jumped back instantly and just saved myself a broken jaw. But the top of his head, while missing my jawbone, caught my nose and blood spurted, as his bristly hair scraped over my cheek, ripping the flesh and tearing loose some of my beard.

I was hurt and staggered, dazed. Dexter came bulling in, again head down, thick arms swinging. He hammered me back against the side of the buckboard which shifted back and forth as the horses jigged in the traces. Skip locked his hands about my throat, banged my head against the hardwood, twisted me about so he could scrape my eyes along the splintery edge of the side plank. Skip wrote the book on dirty tricks.

I didn't aim to be blinded and I reached back with my spurred right boot and ripped it down his leg. I felt the rowel tear through cloth and flesh and dig into bone. Dexter yelled and danced back, involuntarily reaching down to his blood-gushing leg.

I didn't waste the opening. I brought up a knee into his face, felt his nose squish. His large head jerked and I locked both my hands together and slammed then down on to the back of the thick neck. He grunted and went down to one knee. His right hand was fumbling at his belt and I saw the knife sheath for the first time: it had been hidden by the tail of his shirt that had been pulled out of his belt for that purpose.

I took a step back, found my balance and swung a kick into him. It took him high in the chest and he fell, half under the buckboard, between the front and back wheels. Another man would have been unconscious or temporarily paralysed, but Skip Dexter reached his knife and began to fumble for a throwing grip.

I looked at the way his right leg was lying, stretched out in front of the big iron-tyred wheel of the buckboard. *I saw the old man's bony legs poking through the blanket draped across them in his wheel chair, and. . . .*

I jumped forward and yelled, slapping the rump of the nearest horse. Already nervous, eyes rolling, it hit the harness and its companion did the same. The buckboard jerked forward six feet, bounced wildly. Something made a dull, snapping sound like a derringer fired in another room.

But it was instantly drowned by Skip Dexter's screams, his bloody right leg bent now into impossible shape.

The colonel's name was Wingfield and he had the bearing of a professional military man. I hazarded a guess that he might not be entirely happy with his posting as the Reconstruction Director in this part of Texas. Just a hunch and I kept it handy where I might use it to advantage if the chance offered.

But if he was a professional he would do his duty whether he was happy or not. And he didn't seem happy with me as he scanned a paper he held. Steely eyes looked above the edge of the paper and bored into me as I stood there in my dusty rags.They had quite a deal of blood on them now, not all mine.

'This is your home town, McQuade?'

'It is.'

'It is 'sir',' he told me levelly enough. Testing.

'I'm no longer in any army, Colonel.'

He sighed. 'Reb through and through, eh? Yankee-hater from way back. Here to make as much trouble as you can for me.'

'I don't even know you, Colonel. I came home to see my father and to work his ranch if he needed me.'

'I've read something of you, McQuade. We keep track of you Rebs and a Lieutenant Clegg sent me word you and some friends would be arriving here soon. He considers you to be hard men and handy with guns.'

That surprised me. 'The lieutenant and his patrol saved our necks in the Territory. Bunch of Kiowa renegades with some Apache and Comanche thrown in almost had our scalps.'

'So – we Yankees have some use, eh?'

I couldn't make out just which way he was going. One moment I feared he would slap me in jail for brawling and whatever else he could think up by way of charges, the next there was a definite, not 'friendly', maybe 'neutral' attitude.

'Sure did that day, Colonel. We were mighty glad to see Lieutenant Clegg.'

'Now you're home and picking brawls the first time you come to town.'

I debated whether to tell him about Pa and Skip

Dexter. I settled for, 'Skip and me go way back to the schoolyard. He's still a bully and was picking on one of my saddle-mates.'

He glanced at the paper, ran a hand over his short, sandy hair. 'Dennis?'

'We call him Denny. He was blown up by a shell and hasn't been quite right in the head since. He's also about a third of the size of Dexter.'

He gave me a hard look. 'You broke Dexter's legs.'

'Only one: the buckboard jumped forward and the wheel caught him.'

The hard stare didn't waver. 'I understand the buckboard had a little help – 'jumping forward' . . . and your father had both legs broken.'

I nodded. 'Dexter gave him a partly tamed bronc to ride and a saddle that wasn't adjusted properly, either through sloppiness or intentionally.'

The grey eyes narrowed. 'McQuade, you're under my jurisdiction here. I see a few angles to this thing that I don't like . . . and a couple I can understand well enough. Mr Byron has spoken up on your behalf and that fellow from the livery stables—'

'Ash Dillon.'

'Yes, Dillon.' He paused, flapped the paper and set it down, took his time looking up at me again. 'I'm going to take a chance on you, McQuade. I like to think I can judge men pretty well after twenty-five years in the army, and I've learnt to go on first impressions. I've got a damn difficult job here, thanks to my predecessor leaving me a legacy of hatred and non-cooperation. You Texans don't make it any easier. That's to be expected, but even though I sympathize with your attitudes, in part, I still have to cope with them – Reconstruction's not always fair . . .'

I grunted at that but he didn't pause.

' . . . but it's my job to administer it. And I will do the best job I'm capable of. I *need* co-operation, but I won't beg for it; I'll be as hard as I need to be, easy when I can, or I figure it's time to use a velvet glove. But, understand this: the Reconstruction Law will be carried out to the letter, and its penalties for disobeying it will be meted out according to that law, harsh, unfair or otherwise. Do not make the mistake of taking this as softness on my part, McQuade. I'll expect you to obey the rules and I make you responsible for your friends' behaviour, too. You satisfied with that? Or do your Rebel instincts tell you that here's a soft-touch, a chance to bend the rules a little, perhaps more and more, until you're brought before me again?'

'I don't think I'd care for that to happen, Colonel. Thanks. I didn't come home for trouble. Had enough of fighting. Just want to help the old man rebuild his ranch.'

'And it's my job to help rebuild this country that all of us, North *and* South, practically destroyed.' He stood and surprised me by extending his right hand.

I hesitated, then we shook across the desk. The sentry at the door cleared his throat, but some colour drained from his face when Wingfield glared at him.

'Go back to your ranch and get to work, McQuade. I'll have someone check up from time to time.'

'Come yourself,' I invited and he smiled thinly, spread his hands across his cluttered desk.

'Too much paperwork. Good luck, McQuade.'
I left, still not believing I wasn't behind bars.

Kitty cleaned me up and put a light bandage over my ribs where the tool had scraped me. She had a pile of clothes on the counter, guessing my size pretty well, and Toohey, Denny and Morg were selecting what they wanted, Quincey Byron watching carefully, keeping note.

'Even with a broken leg, Skip Dexter can be a dangerous man, Dean,' Kitty said. 'He has friends, both in town and hiding out in the canyons.'

I snapped my head up at that. 'Sounds like Skip's a bigger frog in the pond than I recall.'

'Yes. He somehow managed to stay out of the war and he more or less had a free run here. Since the reconstruction he's had to behave himself, but he still gets what he wants.'

'That Colonel Wingfield said something about a "predecessor"?'

Her face straightened. 'Oh, yes! A strange thing that – a much-scarred Yankee officer arrived with his Reconstruction group, a man called Lawton. They say he was caught in some kind of explosion and that it affected him mentally – he certainly acted like a crazy man here.'

'Wingfield said he left him a "legacy of hatred".'

'Indeed! The whole town hated him. He was cruel and unfair in his administration and finally there were so many complaints that he was relieved of his post and, I believe, court-martialled or invalided out of the army. Either way it was a vast relief for Amarillo

44

and folk living on the high plains.'

'Wingfield seems fair.'

She nodded, face relaxing a little now – this Lawton sure must've stirred things up. 'Yes – its still not easy, being the conquered people, but, as you say, Colonel Wingfield is as fair as his laws allow him.'

We left town soon after that, stopped at the first creek we came to and stripped off, washed and scraped ourselves with coarse sand. Kitty had thoughtfully provided soap and we washed our tangled hair, lathered our beards and used the razor Byron had given us – added it to what we owed, I think. He was kind-hearted enough but he watched the dollars and cents, too, being a businessman.

We hardly recognized each other without the beards, our facial skin where the hair had been show-ing white against the leathery tan. Denny, being sandy-haired, had only had a thin beard and he had left the wispy moustache on. For a while we gave way to an exuberance we hadn't known in years and dunked each other, splashed around, chased each other along the banks as we dried.

It did a lot to relax us and then we dressed in our new, fine smelling clothes. Our battered old campaign hats and worn boots kind of spoiled the picture, but we felt like new men.

In a way we were. For the first time in years of slaughter and daily walking the thin line between life and death, we had a kind of future ahead of us.

It would be whatever we decided to make it.

# CHAPTER 5

# REBUILDING

We had the barn doors fixed by noon the next day and gave Denny the job of painting them. The rest of us went hunting some lodgepole pines for replacing the broken, worn or missing rails and posts on the corrals.

It was good to get into the hard work again, swinging axe and pick, using a crowbar to dig post holes. The sweat ran and the muscles cracked. There had been plenty of times in the army when we had knocked ourselves out, too, but this was different.

We were building something now. Or rebuilding.

Toohey and Morg were just as pleased as I was. It wasn't their spread – nor mine, strictly speaking – but we were working together and towards something that gave satisfaction to feelings long subdued by the endless fighting, running and hiding – wondering whether you were going to wake up to sunrise or a rifle barrel rammed against your head and next instant be hurtled into Eternity.

No matter how tough a man might think he is, that kind of prolonged tension affects him – and not to his benefit.

So we were relaxing, yet working our butts off. It was the enjoyment that benefited us. And, in my case, the apparent softening of the old man.

A couple of times I managed to get him alone without the Chapman woman hanging around. He was civil enough, grudging in his concessions, but he'd always been like that.

'Them boys with you are good workers.'

I smiled to myself: it was a backhand way of telling me I was working to his satisfaction, too. He would never put that into words, though.

'We'll fix the corrals then go hunt up some mustangs. Pa, it still puzzles me how you came to hire Skip Dexter.'

He took his cold pipe from between his teeth and spat. 'Didn't hire him. That son of a bitch Lawton was in charge at the time. He was the one decided who worked where. He sent Skip out to me, said he wanted this place as a payin' spread again so's we could pay our "tribute" to the Reconstruction.'

I nodded slowly, savvying this now. 'Skip practically told me he set you up on a half-broke horse with a saddle that had a worn cinch-strap.'

'I suspected the saddle, but once it was off, hard to prove it hadn't been tightened proper.' He shifted his gaze to me, one of the few times he had looked directly at me since my return. 'Well, he knows what it feels like to have a busted leg now – but you should've done 'em both.'

'I would've if I'd had time to set him up properly.'

He grunted. A silence fell between us.

'Where are the cows, Pa?' I eventually asked quietly.

He kept staring across the yard, watching Denny slap the lime wash on the barn doors. 'Kid's got problems ahead of him, ain't he?'

'We'll take care of him.'

'Can't do it forever.'

'For as long as we can then – Pa, the steers? We had good herds when I took off.'

'When you *quit*!' He wasn't letting me off with anything. 'Sold some to the army. When they couldn't pay, as the war turned bad for us, I just gave 'em what they needed.'

That sounded like him: Texan blood in his veins from way back, ancestors taking their land from the Indians or whoever else was in the way. Hard to the core, and a lot of it had brushed off on me, I guess, too.

'You must've kept some aside.'

He was shrewd. He'd be patriotic till it hurt, but he'd have an eye to the future, too. He took his time answering.

'You recall the Palo Duro?'

Huge canyon country south of here. 'Sure, canyons twisting through the caprock like a nest of snakes. We found a couple that kept good grass almost year round and . . .'

*So that was it! He'd used one of the hidden canyons to stash our best cows.*

That was one of the things about longhorns: their beef wasn't the best, but they took little looking after. If they had grass and water, you could leave them alone for years and they'd breed like rabbits. The herd would grow and could be kept to a manageable size by cutting out bunches in the spring and early summer, selling them off, leaving the rest to graze and multiply. At first they were rounded-up for hides and tallow but Easterners somehow got a taste for beef and that was when the big drives started, mostly to St Louis and Chicago. The war coming along put an end to that and the longhorns, left to themselves on the range, multiplied and spread. Someone estimated the wild longhorns that teemed over Texas ranges after the war numbered as many as five or six million.

*Four bucks in Texas, forty bucks north from Amarillo – a good way north.*

I wasn't much good at figures in school but I could see the opportunity here. The Old Man had looked far enough ahead to prepare for it.

The lean, slab-sided, tough and ornery longhorn was there to be exploited and help us make our fortune.

'Which canyon?' I asked, a mite breathlessly.

He almost smiled, even showed a trace of approval because I'd seen what he had planned all those years ago.

'I'll tell you when you're ready to go get 'em. First the remuda. Then we gotta get some reliable riders.'

'Where's the market, Pa?'

He sucked on the old pipe. 'Charlie Goodnight and Ollie Loving made a drive or two, openin' a trail up through New Mexico and Colorado. Towns there with railheads, Pueblo and Denver seem to be the best.'

I whistled softly. 'Hell, a thousand miles at least!'

'Hell all the way, accordin' to Charlie Goodnight, but worth it. Secret is to get in early; other trails are openin' up to Kansas and such places, too, gettin' crowded, they say. I like to follow in Goodnight and Loving's steps. If you miss the beef trains at Pueblo or Denver, you still got the army posts further west as a market.'

I had to admire the Old Man. Without making too much of my own importance, I knew he must have missed me when I 'quit', and not long after that the war started so he'd have lost most of his good men, and seemed like few or none were coming back. Only me – the bad penny. Toohey, Denny and Morg, were men he hadn't known before.

He'd gotten the bile out of his spleen with me – to some extent, anyway – and now it was time to be McQuades together, get Flag on its feet, despite the Reconstruction restrictions.

'What about the head tax on beeves?'

He did smile! No mistaking it this time!

'Goodnight and Loving are coming north again soon – I've done a deal with 'em. They'll take my cows into their herd and sell 'em, keep a percentage for their trouble. I get the rest of the money and the Reconstruction's none the wiser.'

'They will be when you start using the money to build up this place. Or if you deposit it in the bank.'

'Reckon I'll have somethin' figured by then – Ellie's helpin' me in that direction.'

I stiffened: the first grey edge to the morning had appeared. 'What's she doing here, Pa?' I couldn't keep the sharpness out of my tone and his eyes narrowed.

'You never mind! Your job is to rebuild Flag! I can still run my own life without you buttin' in!'

He was mighty touchy and then, as if on cue,

Eleanor Chapman appeared, smiling, carrying a painted wooden tray with coffee and hot biscuits on it.

'Something to keep things running smoothly, gentlemen,' she said brightly.

I watched the Old Man. His cratered face softened and it reached his eyes. He nodded, 'Thank'ee, Ellie. You are indeed a thoughtful soul.'

He flicked me a glance and I knew that last was more for my benefit than hers. I didn't want to sit and have coffee with her there but I couldn't be so churlish as to just get up and walk away.

'Looks good,' I said, hoping I sounded warmer than I felt.

She gave me a faint smile: she knew I didn't like her, but there was a kind of mild triumph on her face telling me she was there to stay for as long as the Old Man wanted her to. And there was nothing I could do about it.

The biscuits were elegant but I had trouble swallowing them. That, and the message I'd just picked up from her smugness.

Denny had long since finished with the barn doors and we had brought in a couple of dozen mustangs. Toohey was a good bronc-buster and I wasn't too bad, so we had half of them tamed enough to be led around some with empty saddles or burlap sacks containing wet sand across their backs, easing them slowly into feeling and accepting weight to carry.

Both Toohey and me were suffering nosebleeds, sore and stiff from the jarring of busting the horses. So I had Denny take six of them in hand and down to the creek for water and a frolic in the shallows, a roll in the coarse sand of the mid-stream bar. He was so happy to do it I figured he'd be frolicking with them. He was still just a kid, mentally.

Morg was mending the last of the saddles that needed stitching and he watched as he sewed with the clamps under his thigh while we washed up at the well. Our hair dripping, enjoying the afternoon sun on our bare torsos, Toohey and me sat on an old chuckwagon and rolled cigarettes. Morg said he'd leave his smoke till he finished the stitching: his one eye was already watery and red with strain so he'd stop soon.

We talked about what we'd do tomorrow – mostly which horses needed more work on them, decided to toss a coin to see who did the breaking-in. I lost, damnit!

'You fellers feel good enough about things here?' I asked quietly.

We'd been together long enough so I knew there would be no hedging: if they had any bitching to do, they'd do it.

Morgan shrugged. 'I wasn't doin' this, I'd likely still be driftin' – with a hole in my britches and my belly feelin' the same way 'cause there'd be no grub in it.'

'I'm OK.' That said heaps for Toohey.

Good enough. Denny, I knew, was happy here: he even got on well with the Old Man and the Chapman woman.

'We make this drive, we'll all have money in our pockets,' I told them. 'I did a little before and during the war, but you fellers been on a trail drive?'

Morg hadn't but Toohey had, several times. He looked at me kind of shrewdly and asked, 'Before the war, you said?'

*I didn't want to talk about it.* 'Couple. First one not long after I left here. I was just a shaver.'

'How was it?' Why the hell couldn't he leave it alone? I knew he was genuinely interested, but . . .

'Hard, damn hard.' I hoped he'd leave it at that and he did, but he kept looking at me while we smoked down the cigarettes. The old pictures were forming despite efforts to push them back into the greyness of the past.

I was remembering that first cattle drive, a long one up the Shawnee Trail from Brownsville to St Louis. I joined it at San Antonio. My main reason for signing on as wrangler's help and general roustabout was because I had a hankering to see a really big town, maybe even a city.

Instead, I killed my first man between Dallas and Red River Station.

The cook got drunk on Lemon Essence which he had been using to make a dumpling for our supper. He was a queer cuss and the way he'd look at me and sometimes slip an arm about my shoulders or stroke my hips made me uncomfortable. Other times he took a switch to me when I didn't bring in his firewood on time. But this time – I'd never seen him so drunk before although he tippled 'most every day – he dragged me behind the chuckwagon while the others were eating, got me by the back of the neck and threw me to the ground, pushing my face into the dirt.

'Not a word, or I'll slit your scrawny throat!'

I could smell the lemon on his breath and he was breathing like a steer in swamp country. I didn't like the way his free hand was roving over my body. Then cold steel touched my throat and I went rigid.

I was about as scared as I ever remember – and then he put down the knife to fumble at the belt on his trousers. I got that knife, twisted over fast and I'm still not sure if he slipped and fell on the blade, or whether I deliberately rammed it into his chest up to the hilt. Panicked, I stabbed a couple more times but he was already dead. His hot blood was sticky on my hands as I dropped the blade: that's why I don't like knife-fights, I guess, the feel of cold steel slicing into living flesh and the hot blood spurting. . . .

The trail drivers were mighty angry at me – not because I'd killed a man who was trying to abuse me, but because he was *the cook!*

'Now who the hell's gonna feed us?' was the general cry, from the trail boss down to the wrangler.

*I* had to become the trail cook. The boss tried to give me some basic lessons, but he didn't know much and I wasn't so hot and when we got to Caldwell after crossing the Indian Territory they unanimously fired me.

I was barely fifteen years old, a long, long way from home with empty pockets. The War saved me: I bluffed my way into the Confederate Army by boosting my age by a year.

That was my one and only trail drive before the war, though I did several while in uniform, dodging Yankees.

'Denny oughta be back by now,' Morg said

suddenly, and I looked up at the sky: it would be dark soon.

Morg was right and I had a bad feeling, one that had earned my respect over the long, killing years: a hunch that something had happened to the kid while we'd been beating our gums and smoking.

I roped my claybank and began to saddle it. Toohey was doing the same with his sorrel, neither of us speaking.

'Wait here, Morg,' I said swinging aboard and spurring out of the yard, Toohey a couple of lengths behind.

The creek wasn't far in a straight line but you couldn't get there that way unless you were a bird. There was a deal of twisting and turning through sagebrush and grey-green mesquite and a tangle of scrub.

I heard a horse whinny to my left, veered that way, crashed the claybank through screening brush.

Denny was lying half in the creek, his face, streaked with blood, resting on one arm, nose just clear of the muddy water. I could only see two of the horses, on the far bank.

We lifted Denny on to the grass.

He'd been beaten – badly beaten, his face almost unrecognizable, shirt torn and bloodstained, ribs showing bruises in the shape of a boot sole.

Someone had scratched something in the sand on the bar with a stick. There was just enough light left to read it:

*Lousy reb.*

# CHAPTER 6

# HIGH CANYON

A cold wind howled mournfully through the canyon, like a funeral dirge, when I broke my cold camp on the ridge that clung to the side of the lava like a snail on a rock.

In the growing light I had a view of what lay ahead – if I made it down safely. There was the opening to another canyon and I could already see grass and brush just inside the entrance. There would be water in there and both the claybank and I needed it. The canteen had a hollow sound banging against the harness where it hung by its strap from the pommel.

This was the third day and I figured I was closing in on the coyotes who had beaten Denny to a pulp – they'd also stolen the horses he had been watering, except for two. But to hell with the broncs, it was the men I wanted.

Two of them by the tracks. They had made no effort to cover their trail away from the creek.

Would've been a mite hard, mind, driving five half-broke horses through that country.

'Looks like they got plenty of confidence,' Morg allowed grimly. 'Know the country or don't give a damn.'

'Mebbe a little of both,' opined Toohey.

We'd brought Denny back to the spread and here I found out that the Chapman woman was no nurse. Sure, she could bandage a cut, rub arnica into bruises, clean a wound. But when it came to busted ribs, and bleeding from the ears, nose and mouth as in Denny's case, she stepped away.

'I'm sorry – this is beyond me. You'll have to take him in to Amarillo. The army's got a good medical corp.'

She wouldn't look at me, but my eyes bored into her coldly. If she wasn't the nurse we had believed her to be, *just what the hell was she doing here, supposedly looking after the Old Man?*

He was sitting in his wheelchair on the porch, alone, when I went out. Stars were appearing now and he had his pipe going.

'Too bad about the kid . . . any notion who did it?'

'Not yet.'

' "Lousy reb" sounds like Yankees.'

'Meant to sound that way.' He snapped his head around. 'This has Skip Dexter's touch, Pa. He was rousting Denny when I broke it up and we fought. This is likely just the start: getting back at me, using his cronies.'

The Old Man grunted, puffed away thoughtfully. 'I got ammo that'll fit that rimfire of yours – don't matter how I come by it, but you take it with you.'

He knew I was going after whoever had beaten Denny.

And I did, leaving before first light. Toohey would take Denny into town in the buckboard, while Morg stayed on at the ranch. He might have only one eye and one gun but that was all he needed: half a hundred dead Yankees could attest to that.

I went through town with Toohey and Denny, saw him taken into the army infirmary, then went to see Quincey Byron again and strained our relationship some by asking him to outfit me.

'Seems I run credit for half the damn town, Dean!' he growled.

'You know the McQuades always pay their debts, Mr Byron.'

'Is that what you're doing? Going to pay some kind of debt on your friend's behalf?'

'He'd do it for me if he could.'

'That kid!'

'He'd do it for me,' I repeated flatly and felt my face harden. I could see that made him uncomfortable. 'Can you help me out, or not?'

He sighed. 'Just how much grub do you want?'

'We've just had a new delivery, Dad,' Kitty said, suddenly appearing in the curtained doorway that separated the shop from their living area. 'I was visiting Mrs Grahame and her new baby when they brought Denny into the infirmary – the boy's terribly injured.'

Byron nodded OK then and mumbled something,

going back through the curtain.

'Thanks, Kitty.'

Her lovely eyes searched my face. 'I would never recognize you as the easy-going rascal you were when you left here, Dean . . . or do you prefer Stretch these days?'

'Got used to it in the army. Had to get used to a lot of things.'

'Like fighting your friends' battles.'

I merely nodded. She knew how a man was supposed to act and it surprised me. But there was no hesitation in this: Denny or Morg or Toohey would have done the same for me. In fact, Morg and Toohey were champing at the bit at being left behind. We were a close-knit foursome and I hoped we weren't going to be reduced to a trio.

I took time to check with the army medic, but he could only tell me mostly what I already knew: busted ribs, possibly one lung slightly punctured, maybe a fractured skull, and someone had ground a bootheel into the back of Denny's right hand.

I quit town fast, grub sacks bouncing as I headed for the high country. Now I was closing in on the sons of bitches who had done this to Denny.

I had a bandoleer slung across my chest, every loop filled with a .44/.40 rimfire cartridge, the Henry's 14-round magazine filled, with one extra in the breech.

I would use every bullet I had and then go in swinging the rifle by its hot barrel if I had to. But these animals were not going to ride out of that canyon.

I was sure that's where they were. I had come to the ledge near sundown last night and, dismounted, leading the weary claybank, I'd caught a shaft of dying amber light hitting a clear patch between the lava rock below. It was reflected from a flat slab and struck at a low angle, showing clearly the indentation of several horses' hoofs.

When I was settled on the ledge, I refrained from smoking although the craving for tobacco was strong. I didn't want to spoil my sense of smell.

Woodsmoke reached me, and a side dish of broiling beefsteak or maybe antelope chops made my belly growl.

I salivated and munched on cold, stale biscuit and some dried-out cheese. *Eat well, you murdering bastards!*

The condemned's last meal. . . .

I ground-hitched the claybank amongst some rocks a few yards from the canyon entrance, had the last of my water, and went in with the rifle at high port across my chest. The Colt sat snugly in my crude holster on my left hip, butt foremost. I could draw it pretty fast: I'd practised and a couple times put that practice to use. I was good enough.

The sun was rising now, lifting a few tendrils of mist that I could use as cover. At the entrance, I crouched against the rock, pushed my hat to the back of my head and looked around carefully. The camp-fire was going again and this time I smelled bacon and coffee. *They were living damn well!*

But not for much longer.

I eased into the canyon, pressing close to the eastern wall, utilizing the shadow it cast. I crept closer to the camp where I could see the two of them sitting on a deadfall, cooking their breakfast.

As I took one more step, I found out there were three of them, not just two.

Sure, I'd followed tracks of two riders all the way from Flag Creek, but there must have been a third man either waiting here where they were supposed to lead me, or riding parallel to their trail some distance away, waiting to move in on me.

I would never have made such a mistake in the army – not and lived to talk about it, anyway.

The shot beat at my ears at the same instant as the slug gouged dust from the rock beside my head. Broken bits stung that side of my face, making me lurch involuntarily. The move took me out of the shadow and the ambusher triggered his second shot. He got me in the lower left leg and it collapsed under me, throwing me even more into the open.

But that gave me one advantage: I landed on my back, still clutching the rifle at ready position and, looking up, I saw the shooter. His head and shoudlers were silhouetted against the fiery sky and the old reflexes cut in. The butt of the Henry was snug against my shoulder in an instant and the trigger let off smoothly under my curled finger. Before the ejected shell case had reached the top of its trajectory, I had a second cartridge in the breech and I fired that, too.

The man up there grew fast, head, shoulders and torso stretched into waist and hip and finally kicking legs as he was jerked upright by my bullets. He flapped his arms all the way down but he couldn't fly worth spit and crumpled amongst the rocks four or five yards to my left.

I knew I wouldn't have to go through the routine of feeling for a pulse.

By now the other two had decided to skip breakfast and were hammering at me with their weapons. The numbness was going from my leg and my riding boot was filling with blood.

I dragged myself into some cover, rolled back under a cutbank so I could try my leg with weight on it. It hurt but held. I tore off my neckerchief and bound it over the wound, unable to tell if the bullet was still in there. But it was bleeding plenty.

The cutbank soon became untenable, bullets ricocheting. The killers had separated, making two targets for me to worry about, but also putting themselves in position to rake my shelter in a crossfire.

They were good and I figured these were ex-army men, too. I had done my share of belly-crawling during the war and found I hadn't forgotten a thing when I moved position. I was close to the ground as any snake, in fact so close my belt buckle scooped sand and dirt down the inside of my trousers, spilling it against my belly.

A bullet sent my hat spinning and another chipped a rock and gave me a cut above my right eye. The blood it spilled made sighting a hard chore and I blotted it up several times with the shoulder of my shirt before I got a bead.

A man in a grey shirt made a dash between two boulders up there. I figured he aimed to climb the second one and so give himself a high advantage. He never made it. I led him by only a few inches and he ran smack into the bullet I sent to greet him. He twisted and spun away, almost but not quite dropping his rifle.

But he was down, writhing still, but down. His pard was nowhere to be seen – *Wait!* There he was, already down flat like me, snaking around the base of one of those boulders, pushing his rifle out ahead of him. His mistake: the sun flashed along the barrel before he could drop it down to ground level. He must have known I'd seen it because he started to back-pedal. My next two shots hurried him along, but I swore when I realized I hadn't managed to hit him.

I needed to set the sight scale. No need to allow for windage in here – or was there? That mournful wind was still howling. I couldn't feel it but when I looked more closely, I saw a faint haze of dust rising out to the left, likely the heat of the rising sun waking up small wind-devils.

Three fast shots raking my cover made me hurry. A quick guessed-at adjustment, swing the barrel down towards the pall of smoke. Give him a chance to fire once more – the sudden spurt of smoke issuing at that instant would pinpoint him and . . .

The Henry kicked against my shoulder and I levered, put two more quick shots over that way. I hit him this time, but he still managed to get up and, crouched double, limping, one arm dangling, he made a run for a space between two rocks. He dropped and I couldn't see him: must be a scooped-out hollow there.

Limping, I made my way along the shadowed eastern wall. He must know I was there by now. But I think I'd given him cause for worry with that last volley. Sweating, my leg hurting and taking some of my attention now despite efforts to push the pain aside, I straightened – and looked right into the muzzle of a big-bore Spencer carbine. My Henry's long barrel, great for extra accuracy, was a curse right at this moment.

There wasn't enough room for me to bring it around. So I let it fall, and the clatter distracted him for a moment as I let myself roll forward, under the Spencer as it roared in that flat thunder it was known for. I snatched my Colt, twisted like a cat, and thumbed the hammer twice. I glimpsed a beard-shagged face under a dark-brown hat's wide brim, saw the eyes fly wide – an instant before my slugs smashed the face into something shapeless and very bloody.

I hurt my leg rolling off the rock and grabbed it as I hitched myself past the dead man, remembering the other one I'd shot earlier and how he had still writhed before dropping out of sight.

Just as well I did. A handgun boomed above me and to my right. The lead flicked at the loose sleeve of my new shirt and that made me mad. I only fired one shot but it ricocheted into the chest of the wounded man and knocked him off his rock as if a mule had kicked him.

There wasn't much life left in him when I limped across, covering him with the still-cocked Colt. I recognized him: Dal Spinney, one of Skip Dexter's cronies even at school.

He recognized me, too: well, I guess that had to be, because he must have known who he was leading into this death trap.

'You look about as bad as the day I licked you under the apple tree in Flannigan's orchard, Dal.'

He managed to spit – blood-coloured.

'When you think Skip'll be able to walk and do his own dirty work?'

'Too – too soon for . . . your . . . likin'!'

'Yeah, mebbe. You do the kickin?' He knew I was referring to Denny and he was suddenly wary through his pain, shook his head.

'Was . . . Lobo.'

So that's who the other one was: there hadn't been enough of his face left for me to recognize him a couple of minutes ago. Another sidekick of Skip Dexter's.

'They should've named him coyote. You don't look too good, Dal. Guess I'll have to tell Skip myself that you made a mess of the deal. Likely makes you lucky, anyway, him being the bad-tempered cuss he is if he don't get his own way.'

I stood, favouring the wounded leg. He lifted a clawed hand. 'Don' – don't leave me like this, McQuade!'

'No choice, Dal. I'm hit and bleeding plenty. Got those hosses to round-up and get back to Flag. Nothing I can do for you anyway . . . 'less you got some water?'

He gestured to his camp and I found a couple of canteens, both near full. I swigged, returned and gave him a drink. But he vomited it up and while I was tearing up some brush to make him a headrest for his last minutes, he went into a violent fit of coughing and died.

It wasn't an easy ride back.

In fact, I didn't make it all the way. Rounding-up those half-broke horses turned out to be a mighty big chore and coming on top of digging graves for the three bushwhackers, and burying them, it took a deal out of me.

My leg had eased-up bleeding but it was sore as hell and I guessed the slug was still in there. Apparently, it hadn't broken the bone, but must be lodged in or near a muscle. I had to ride with the boot dangling free of the stirrup and couldn't put any weight on it at all.

I only managed to catch two of the missing broncs – the others were in devilish mood and played hell with me, letting me get within rope-tossing range and then ducking their heads or kicking up their heels – either way leaving me with a dangling rope and empty noose.

So I said to hell with them and started back.

Fever was setting in and I don't recall too much of the ride. But there was a time when the sun was beating down on my hunched-over back and I realized I was clinging to the claybank's neck, unable to sit upright any longer in the saddle.

Things were kind of blurry and I was shocked when I lifted one of the canteens I'd taken from the camp in the high canyon and found only a mouthful of water left in it.

Got a bigger shock when I went for the second canteen and realized it was already empty.

I didn't know where the horses I'd been driving were. I was just glad the claybank was under me.

But not too much later on, I was under it, moaning in the dust, trying to reach up and grab a stirrup so as to pull myself on to my feet. *Foot, McQuade – you only have one good leg to support you. . . .*

Yeah.

Then I heard saddle gear and harness and through a grey cloud saw moving figures.There was an exchange of some words I couldn't make out. But one thing rang clearly through my head:

*Yankees! I'd run into a Yankee patrol!*

Fumbling, I dragged at my Colt.

# CHAPTER 7

# YANKEES GALORE

The patrol was under Lieutenant Clegg, the Yankee who had rescued us from the renegade attack in Indian Territory.

He took me into Amarillo and I found myself a few beds away from Denny in the infirmary. The doctor had cut the ball out of my leg, told me there was no permanent damage, and I would be walking without the aid of a stick in a week or so.

Denny – well, he hadn't yet regained consciousness and the sawbones was reluctant to hazard a guess when he might do so – or even *if* he would do so.

'Do the best you can, Doc. He's got no kin and had a helluva tough time during the war.'

'Him and thousands of others, McQuade. But be assured we will put him together if it's at all possible.'

Clegg was waiting at the door. 'Colonel wants to see you.'

Clegg seemed more serious than when I'd last seen him up in the Territory.

'You and me – we better stop meeting like this,' I said, seeing if I could lighten him up: that deadpan look worried me, like something was wrong, badly wrong.

'You just don't like being rescued by Yankees.'

The lightness just touched his words, but there was no hint of a smile as he took my free arm to help me: I wasn't yet used to using a walking stick.

He got me a chair in Wingfield's office and stood stiffly to one side. The colonel didn't appear to be in a light-hearted mood, either.

'There's no room for vigilantes in the Reconstruction plan, McQuade,' he said, straight from the shoulder. 'You went after three men and wilfully killed them.'

'What should I've done?'

'I don't believe I have to tell you. You're smart enough to know damn well.'

I sighed. 'There was no time, Colonel. You know the winds that blow through the high country. I'd've lost the tracks coming in to report things to you first.'

'You came into town with your friend.'

'Sure. Wanted to see him right. Then I went to the general store and begged some grub and a blanket roll to outfit me for the trail. . . . Those men were waiting for me, had an ambush all set up, stole our horses. Unwritten law in Texas that a man hunts down horse and cattle-thieves, Colonel. Strings 'em up on the spot, or trades lead. It was a fair shoot-out – if you want to call three against one fair.'

Wingfield's set expression didn't change, but I could see something changing in his eyes: they were no longer friendly.

'I have no use for "unwritten" laws, McQuade.' He lifted a brown leather-covered book and gestured to me with it. 'These are the only laws that apply here – *written* especially for the Reconstruction – and I will see them obeyed.'

Clegg lightly kicked one leg of my chair and his hip sort of nudged me: warning me not to push the colonel any further. I let Wingfield stare me down, then spread my hands.

'Colonel, I've had six years of going out and killing the enemy when he does me, or my men, some harm – I can't just stop.' His face started to change and I added quickly, 'But I'll sure try damn hard to next time.'

Clegg smothered a sort of cough, and Wingfield dragged his gaze across the lieutenant before returning it to me. 'I don't want there to be a next time, McQuade. You've been back a matter of weeks and I've had trouble enough from you. I've been lenient because I need to have as much approval of the people I'm trying to rehabilitate as possible. You may not consider Yankees very smart, but I'm smart enough to know if I disciplined you harshly for what you've done, I'll only make more trouble for myself than . . than –' did his lips twitch just a mite then? – 'than you can shake a stick at.'

I smiled crookedly. 'Careful, Colonel, you're picking up the Texas jargon.'

'If it'll make my rules better understood, I'll talk in

70

Chinese if necessary – now, do you understand me, McQuade?'

'I do, Colonel – and I'm grateful. Because all I really want to do is rebuild Flag and see my father walk again.'

'Then get on with it – and work within the boundaries of Reconstruction. That's all I ask. I have to be harsh at times, and make no mistake I *will* be when harshness is called for, but I'm also here to help. I don't believe in ruining people and then expect them to rebuild what has been taken away from them. I think we need more co-operation – on both sides. Men like you can help bring this about, McQuade – your father, too. I'd like you to tell him that.'

Clegg saw me out and at the gate of the fort said, 'You understand what he was saying to you?'

'Not all us Texans are dumb, Lieutenant. He's played fair with me, told me he'll continue to do so as long as I play fair with him.'

Clegg nodded, scratching his moustache. 'I hope you can be depended on to do that, McQuade.' I looked at him sharply. 'Because I'll be the one the colonel will send to bring you into line.'

I smiled crookedly. 'Already said we have to stop meeting the way we have been.'

'That part's up to you, so stay out of trouble. . . .'

I don't know if there is such a thing as a decent enemy, but I felt I'd just met a couple of them who came mighty close. I limped back towards town. I knew I'd been lucky; Wingfield could have thrown me in jail, or worse.

*

Kitty wanted me to stay overnight at the store – I could see Mr and Mrs Byron weren't keen on the idea, so I declined as gracefully as I could.

'Thanks anyway, folks, but I need to get back to see what's been happening at Flag.'

At the door I turned to Kitty and asked if she would let me know how Denny was doing. 'We might be on round-up so I won't have much chance to get into town.'

She looked alarmed. 'Round-up?' she almost whispered the word. 'Stretch, if Flag has cattle the administration doesn't know about. . . .'

'What cattle?' I said quickly, cursing my loose lips. 'I meant rounding-up mustangs. Pa has a notion of selling some to the army.'

It was feeble enough and I didn't like lying to her, but she looked relieved and accepted it. She shook my hand almost shyly.

'I hope you'll be able to get back into town again soon.'

'I'll be trying.'

And I meant that.

I told the Old Man what Wingfield had said and he grunted, stared at me in silence for a long spell. I let the silence drag on until he said, 'You look worried.'

I shrugged. 'I think Wingfield was telling me more than I realized at the time. Pa, I think he has a hunch that there're Flag steers back in those canyons somewhere. I believe he'll come down on us like a Red

River flood if we try to dodge this damn head tax.'

He grunted and it could have meant anything.

'It sounds trivial, a few cents a head,' he said after a while. 'Multiply that by the million or so longhorns estimated to be runnin' wild in this neck of the woods and you've got a fortune – if you're on the collectin' end. If you're on the *payin'* end, tax on even a few thousand head will send any spread I know in the Panhandle dead broke.'

'Hell! Are we holding many?'

'I dunno how many there are now, but there was a few hundred when we drove 'em into the canyons and closed 'em off just after war started. Kept some out to sell or give to the army so's they wouldn't be too suspicious – I had a hunch beef would be important after the war, no matter who won, and wanted some I could use for restockin'.'

'When's the Goodnight-Loving herd due?'

'Waitin' for word.'

'They'd be in a helluva lot of trouble if they got caught running our cows in with theirs, wouldn't they?'

'Ol' Charlie Goodnight's pretty sharp – he'll have somethin' worked out. He was tryin' to negotiate a deal with the Yankees down his way: drive the beef up north, sell it, then pay head tax. Think they were listenin', but only if he "donates" a certain number of beeves to the army. He can afford to, but dunno whether the deal came off.'

It sounded pretty good to me. *Selling your steers first then paying the tax: made a lot of sense from our point of view.*

I wondered if maybe smaller-time outfits like Flag could win themselves a similar deal. If I could catch Winfield in a reasonable mood, it might be possible.

Anyway, another visit to town would be a good chance to see Denny – *all right, and Kitty Byron.*

I was on the porch, on my way to the corrals, when I caught the Old Man struggling to push himself up so he could reach his pipe which someone had placed on a small wall shelf with his tobacco, just out of his reach.

'I'll get it,' I said and, as I handed it to him, saw he was breathing like someone who'd run a mile, I helped him arrange the blanket across his lap. *And felt the bony thinness of his upper legs and knees.* 'Pa, you been getting any exercise?'

'Exercise?' he echoed, frowning. 'I can't hardly get my legs to move let alone stand.'

I went to the door and called into the house. 'Mrs Chapman! Bring my father's crutches.' I refused to call her Ellie: didn't want to get that familiar.

Looking puzzled and a little tight-lipped, no doubt because of my tone, she came out carrying his crutches. She looked at me coldly. 'They were just inside the door.'

'All right, but keep them where Pa can reach 'em. He needs to use them every day. Strengthen his leg muscles.'

'Oh? Is that your considered opinion, Dean? I wasn't aware you had a medical background.'

'You get to know things in the army,' I answered curtly. 'But he'll never stand a chance of walking if he doesn't build up those muscles – they're just wasting away! What the hell kind of nurse are you?'

The Old Man stirred and fury darkened her face. 'A damned good one!' she snapped.

I suppose it was uncalled for, but I couldn't help it: she riled me just by being there and I wasn't sure why. I sensed she was after something, and I knew the Old Man was kind of soft on her, so that must make him vulnerable by my reasoning.

I jumped when he whacked me across the shoulders with one of his crutches. 'Don't you speak that way to Ellie!'

I rubbed my arm as she said, putting on a smile and a long-suffering look, 'It's all right, Hiram. A nurse gets used to uncalled-for abuse—'

'Well, you don't need to get used to it here! You apologize, damn you!'

He was snorting and breathing hard, his rheumy eyes starting out of his head. 'It was uncalled for, Mrs Chapman. I've got no excuse – I'm sorry.' I was afraid he'd have a fit.

She sensed I was doing it for the Old Man's sake but she nodded: it was good enough apparently.

'But,' I added before she could speak, 'the doctor in Amarillo told me to walk as much as I could on my leg as long as it didn't hurt. He said muscles wasted quickly without regular exercise. I asked him about Pa and he said it would help him to get what exercise he could. With leg muscles able to support him and his movements, he stands a better chance of being able to walk again.'

The army doctor hadn't said any such thing, not

about Pa, anyway, because I hadn't mentioned him, but he had told me to exercise my wounded leg. I figured Ellie Chapman wouldn't want to go against 'proper' medical advice.

'Well, I suppose it *could* help,' she conceded. 'We'll work out a daily schedule, Hiram.' She smiled, patted his shoulders and pulled the blanket aside.

We both helped him to his feet, him cussing all the way. We found one crutch was slightly longer than the other, so I arranged with Morg to adjust it, then limped on to the corrals with my own stick.

Denny hadn't yet regained consciousness and the doctor admitted he was worried about the kid's chances now: he was developing a cough and he was afraid pneumonia might set in and finish him off.

Spirits down around my boot-heel level, I went to see the colonel and slowly told him of my idea.

Wingfield listened to my proposition, was silent when I'd finished putting it to him.

I was too impatient and jumped in again. 'None of us has any money to pay taxes, Colonel. You said yourself it was futile to ruin a man and then expect him to pay taxes and rebuild his spread.'

'You have a point, McQuade. But I'd have to send someone along with the herd to supervise, make sure the head count was correct and the tax calculated accurately.'

'Shouldn't be a problem.' Although I knew there were some ranchers around this neck of the woods who sure wouldn't like a Yankee riding along on round-up or trail drive. 'One other thing, Colonel: most trail herds can lose up to half their cows on a

76

bad drive because of waterless stretches, Indians, rustlers maybe, prairie fires, stampedes. It would need to be a headcount after we reach trail's end, for calculating taxes.'

He stared at me levelly then smiled just a little. 'You've thought carefully about this, I see, but you're loading things in your favour, McQuade.'

'I see it as playing fair, Colonel. You wouldn't expect a man to pay head tax on a steer that's already dead, would you?'

'The way it works, the tax is on how many cows a man *owns* – if any die afterwards, that's his misfortune.'

I wasn't sure how far I could push him on this, only appeal to his sense of fair play, and he seemed to have a fairly well-developed one.

So we swung it back and forth and in the end he agreed to only charge the tax on the number of steers sold at the railhead.

Which was damn generous of him, really, when other Yankee administrators were sinking in the boot at every chance so as to beat down the 'lousy rebs'. And keep them beat down.

'But – one time only, McQuade. I'll make a deadline for moving herds out,' he added, eyes turning hard as they watched my face. 'Say, two months from now. Any cattle still in my jurisdiction after that time will be taxed, *where they stand*. If they're later driven to market and some are lost. . . .' He spread his arms, shaking his head. 'Too bad, I'm afraid.'

It was the best I could hope for, in fact better than I'd hoped for. He was bending the rules because he

77

was a fair-minded man at heart. I didn't know what kind of trouble he could get himself into, but that had nothing to do with me.

Just as long as he agreed to taxing us only on what we delivered to the railhead and sold.

I went to Byron's and told Kitty and her father about the negotiation. Quincey Byron pursed his lips.

'Well, he sure is a better administrator than that Scarface Lawton – he'd have had you shot for even suggesting such a scheme, Dean.'

'I'm kinda glad I got here after he'd gone.'

'How about a crew? You'll need good, experienced men for a trail drive.'

That was one of my worries. 'We'll find men some-where.'

'Not around here.' Byron was firm about that. 'Plenty of roustabouts who'll try anythin', but experi-enced riders. . . .' He shook his head slowly.

Kitty saw me to the door and I was surprised she took my arm. 'Getting used to the walking stick, I see.'

'I don't want to get used to it – sooner I can throw it away the better.'

She said she would walk with me as far as the dress-maker's – it was on the way to the livery where I'd left the claybank. Outside the barber's we turned to cross the street and suddenly there was a loud rumble of wheels, shouting, and horses whinnying, rearing up only yards from us. I yanked the startled girl back. She stumbled into my arms.

*I had no complaints.*

When the team settled, I saw they were hitched to a buckboard driven by a bullet-headed, bearded man I'd never seen before. But sitting alongside, one leg made massive by its plaster cast and resting on the edge of the footboard, was Skip Dexter. He was grinning widely, but it was more a rictus than anything, and his eyes were sparkling, but with undisguised hatred. Kitty clung tightly to my arm.

'Need to watch how you go, McQuade, 'specially when you got that li'l beauty hangin' on your arm.' He leaned his gross body forward a little, made a sucking noise and ran a wet tongue around his lips. 'Sure is prime, ain't she?'

Kitty's grip tightened and I flexed a muscle to let her know I knew how frightened she was.

'You're the one needs to take it easy, Skip. How's the leg?' I tapped the cast with my walking stick and for a moment alarm showed in Skip's eyes. 'Face is healing well. Can hardly see you'd been in a brawl.'

He didn't like my reminding him of the fight. He glared and deliberately shifted his gaze to Kitty and leered. Her grip tightened once more.

'Oh, I'm comin' along OK. Us Dexters are pretty damn tough – might do some good to remember that.'

'I'll be sure to, but you'll need to be tougher than your sidekick Dal Spinney, and his pards.'

Dexter's face went grey, mouth tightening. The bearded man just sat there, waiting for orders, or not much interested, it was hard to tell. Dexter's hand on the seat rail was white-knuckled.

'I ain't finished with you, McQuade! That's all I got to say!'

'And that's plenty,' I said, and pulled Kitty back swiftly as he nudged the bearded man who whipped-up the team pronto. The horses whickered and lunged into the harness. The buckboard scraped by so close the iron wheel rim splintered the edge of the boardwalk. Folk who had been watching, all turned their gazes to me.

'Oh, Dean! Please be careful! Skip Dexter's a – a dreadful man and a very sore loser.'

'Yeah.' That seemed sufficient by way of answer.

My leg was throbbing but I rode carefully on the way home, avoided arroyos and places where timber was thicker than normal. But it seemed Skip hadn't sent any of his men to set up another ambush.

Likely they would keep any further attempts at killing me for out on the range.

There were strange horses in the corrals when I arrived at Flag and I saw three men in shabby clothes standing in the doorway of the barn where Morg was dubbing some boots with neat's-foot oil. Toohey was fitting brass rings to a new set of harness straps Morg had made.

The men turned as I approached, Henry swinging in one hand, thumb on the ear of the hammer, the Colt loose in its holster.

'By Godfrey,' said one, a middle-aged redhead with a dimple in his chin like he had been hit with a meat cleaver. 'If that ain't li'l Dean McQuade all growed-up! An' he don't even recognize me!'

But I did – after a minute. 'Red Kimborough – last I saw of you, you were flying through the air after a bobtailed buckskin mare got tired of feeling your weight on her swayback.'

He grinned, wagged a knobbly finger at me. 'Just as sassy, mebbe more so, than when you was a shaver.' We gripped hands. 'Hear they call you Stretch now – can see why.'

'Glad you made it through the war, Red. Taken you a long time to get back.'

'Yeah – little trouble here and there. Here, meet two pards who know how to work cows: big one with the buck teeth we call Bucky – can't think why. That short-assed feller with all the curls hangin' under his hat goes by the moniker of Curly.'

Curly, of course, was bald and about an inch taller than me, heavier, too.

But I didn't care how he looked: he and Bucky and Red were cowhands, and the chance of making that long trail drive had just come three steps closer.

# CHAPTER 8

# MAVERICKS

'God almighty!'

The exclamation came out involuntarily as I reined down on the rim of the canyon I had been searching for for a day and a half. Morg and Red were with me and their comments were more pungent than mine when they looked at the scene below.

It was one of the biggest canyons on the caprock, one the Old Man had found many years ago and nurtured secretly, bringing it into full use just after the war started. Here was where he had hidden his herds of longhorns, built a log fence across the narrow opening and camouflaged it with bushes. Over the years, the bushes and grass had grown up and no one would know the fence was there unless they rode into it.

That wasn't likely, because they'd have to find the canyon entrance in the first place. And even with the crude map the Old Man had drawn me it had taken us till noon of the second day before we located the place.

Morg had the sharpest hearing – perhaps the body compensating for some damage to one of the other senses, in his case, the loss of an eye. He had said mid-morning he thought he had heard the lowing of cattle. Hard to tell up here where the wind moaned and whistled through the caprock.

But we were looking for cows so we concentrated our search and here we were.

The biggest canyon on the caprock was wall to wall with longhorns of various size and age.

'Must be close to a coupla thousand,' Red commented, and I looked at him.

'You were still working for Pa when he hid these?'

Red shook his head. 'Nah – I'd joined the army. Lem Burgess was here and we met up on the road at Cross Keys, Indiana, and he told me the Old Man had hid his herds, afeared the army would grab 'em without compensation or somethin'. But he never went into details. Lem was killed soon after.'

'Know what happened to the other cowhands who left Flag to go to war?' I asked, seeing the memories forming behind his eyes.

'Huh? Not all – Rio deserted, I heard, and someone said they'd run him down in the desert and buried him up to his neck then rode off. Jimbo Hackett was wounded: I seen him in a hospital camp, but I dunno whether he made it back or not. Dunno anythin' about the rest.'

I nodded, folded my hands on the saddlehorn,

looking at those milling cows as they crowded each other at graze. 'We found this lot just in time. Canyon won't support 'em for much longer. They've got to be moved, trail drive or not.'

'Gonna need a bigger crew than we've got,' Red allowed.

He was right. I figured there were between 1,500 and 2,000 head, a lot of beef on the hoof. With a remuda for at least a dozen riders, three mounts apiece, chuckwagon, supply wagon and camp-out gear we were going to be a major outfit on the Goodnight-Loving Trail. Or any trail.

'Well, Goodnight and Loving'll have their crew,' Morg said.

'And their lot of cattle,' I pointed. out. 'Besides, Pa's heard nothing, doesn't even know for sure Goodnight and Loving are coming this season. They've had them floods down south where they are, you know. Heard it was like an inland sea in parts.'

'How many spreads are still goin' hereabouts?' Red Kimborough asked suddenly. 'I mean big and small.'

'Well, Flag's the biggest. Toby Jensen is trying to put his T Bar J back on the map; I saw the Swede in Byron's store stocking-up on cattle dip so he must be working his spread again. Across the ridge there's Williams, with Hanrahan right next door, brothers-in-law – they married twin sisters. . . . The rest are outlying, backing up into the ranges to the north.'

'Hell, we got plenty of trail hands,' Red said, and Morg and me looked at him quizzically. 'Simple – get 'em to pool their cows with Flag's and ride along or send whoever they got to spare. We could manage a herd of three thousand no trouble.'

I wondered how come I hadn't thought about such a plan. It made a lot of sense: there had been plenty of co-operation between the spreads before the war, so why shouldn't there still be the same? Mutual benefit and Wingfield's promise to charge tax only on those cows that made it all the way to the sale yards . . . that was the answer.

But the Old Man was the stumbling block.

Seems that while the war was on and the spreads were short-handed, some barely managing to hang on, he had taken advantage and bought up a few small ones cheap, adding them to Flag. The ranchers hadn't liked his methods: truth was, the McQuades had been powerful enough in the Panhandle all along, but that didn't mean we were well liked by everybody. Nothing bad enough to cause a feud or anything, but they saw Flag, meaning Pa, as a land-grabber, and some of the small-timers who had tangled with him had long memories.

'It won't work,' he growled at me when I told him what we figured to do. 'They won't co-operate with Flag.'

'Mebbe not with you,' I said heatedly, now I'd found out about what he had done. 'And can't say I blame 'em, but I knew some of their boys, fought alongside 'em, seen some of 'em die. I think I could get them to listen.'

He stared at me with those shrewd grey eyes. 'You're enjoyin' this.'

'What? Trying to get Flag back on its feet as a

paying proposition? Damn right I am.'

'Buildin' up what you figure will be your legacy?' he asked quietly and I stiffened, frowned.

The Chapman woman was there by his chair, helping him settle into it after he'd finished his walk with his crutches.We had him walking the porch, end to end, twenty, thirty times, twice a day now. She gave me a half smile but said nothing.

'I don't look at it that way,' I told the Old Man shortly. 'Flag's my home and I want it paying its way.'

'Your home? After quittin' eight years ago, now you want to claim it as *home* again?'

'What the hell's the matter with you?' I demanded, not understanding his hassling. 'The war held me up, or I'd've been back a year after I left.'

'You say. But don't matter: you owe me, boy! Leavin' me the way you did! Fixin' up Flag is your obligation.'

*So that was how he saw it? Or someone had told him that was the way to look at it.*

I glanced at the woman as she fussed with his rug, set his crutches in the leather holding straps Morg had made and I'd fixed to the porch rail near where he liked to park his wheelchair.

'I know my obligations, Pa,' I said slowly, standing. 'Mrs Chapman, if you'll pack me a couple of grub-sacks, I'll start riding around the other spreads and see if any of them are interested in joining the trail drive.'

'Wastin' your time,' the Old Man growled, packing his pipe bowl.

'You better hope I'm not – Wingfield finds all

those longhorns up in Beehive Canyon after his deadline and we'll be flat broke, have to sell up to pay the damn head tax.'

'Well, get on with it then!'

*Cantankerous old coot!*

Anyway, he was wrong. The smaller ranchers might not have forgiven Pa for his land-grabbing but they were desperate enough and smart enough to see this was their one and only chance. Most had small herds, a couple not admitting to having some cows hidden away, but it was easy to see they had. All but two agreed to throw in their lot with Flag on the one big trail drive. And after we started round-up, and bringing the steers down into the holding pastures, those two changed their minds and joined as well.

Each ranch would be responsible for branding their own cows and they would earn payment on the sale of however many remained at the end of the trail. Grub and transport expenses were to be shared, taken out of a pool according to how many men each ranch provided. Those who brought horses to add to our growing remuda would also be paid a premium.

It looked mighty good on paper and we were all eager to get the herd together and the wagons greased and repaired, iron-tyred wheels renewed and teams shod.

The Panhandle literally hummed with activity and Wingfield approved, although Yankees still hassled folk here and there and complaints were rife. But there was no real problem with the Reconstruction – except it was *there*, of course, and even the fools knew there was no changing *that.*

In the midst of it, Denny returned, looking wan and thin as a matchstick, talking and thinking more slowly than before. But he was alive, and began to fill out on Eleanor Chapman's cooking. He helped the Old Man mostly, did round-the-yard chores, and he was happy, specially when the woman allowed him to tend her vegetable and flower garden.

We heard, too, that Skip Dexter's leg was out of plaster and he was getting around on crutches, drinking in the bars again, letting it be known that he had plenty to square away with me. . . .

Byron's general store had some rocks thrown through their street display windows by a bunch of drunks – mostly Dexter's friends or hangers-on – and Ash Dillon had a fire in his livery, but luckily it was small and put out before any real damage was done.

Lieutenant Adam Clegg was investigating, but apparently was making little progress. No one knew anything, or were too scared to say.

And then Clegg began to notice something: all these mysterious mishaps were to people who had helped the McQuades in one way or another. Like the blacksmith who had set aside other work to make a set of iron tyres for our chuckwagon – he had his bellows slashed one night: replacing them was no easy matter. The Swede's ranch had fences torn down and his few cows stampeded into a bog after he and his wife took it upon themselves to bring our round-up crew grub a couple of days running to save us going back to Flag – that kind of thing. Josh Taylor who went out of his way to deliver us some bales of wire and post-hole digging tools was found beaten and robbed in an alley. Tambo, who brought our mail, was waylaid, beaten, and the mailbag destroyed.

And Skip Dexter was back riding again, awkwardly, but making daily progress, bullying as if to make up for lost time, the chip on his shoulder bigger than ever.

No proof of course, but he was crowing about all these things happening to people in the Amarillo saloons.

'Couldn't happen to nicer folk!' he declared.

Clegg braced him straight out and got nothing but denials and smug smirks. And a challenge to prove he was responsible for the incidents.

'I still think he's behind this,' the lieutenant told me and I agreed.

'I'm sure he is, the son of a bitch,' I said grimly.

Clegg shook his head when he saw my face. 'Don't do it, Stretch. You go after him now and it'll be just what he wants. He'll play it by the book, complain to Wingfield, demand you be brought to heel. And a court case'll delay the drive until after the deadline and you know what that means.'

'Would Wingfield enforce the head tax under those circumstances?'

'He'd have to. He's proclaimed it in writing on those notices all around the county and, you recollect, he says, "no excuses for evasion will be considered".'

I doubled the nighthawks on the holding pastures where the herd was kept while it grew larger day by day.

The round-up went on and some of the Yankees sent out to watch we weren't manipulating the head count pitched in and seemed to enjoy themselves. It was all new to them.

But Skip was too smart to hit the herd in a raid while the Yankees were there: instead there was a brushfire one night – and that started a stampede.

The steers went through the first lot of fences as if they weren't there and one of Jensen's men, on nighthawk duty, was thrown and broke a collarbone. We lost two horses to those damn raking horns and were lucky it wasn't worse.

Our outer fences were stronger and the herd came up against them, bawling and howling and climbing each others' backs, ripping their horns into anything within reach, the posts creaking, the rails beginning to lean outwards. If they got through and scattered again, we would never have time to round them up and clear the county by the deadline.

Old Toohey saved the day – or the night. He forced the tangled, brawling steers into a 'wheel'. Something he had picked up during his pre-war travels. I'd never seen it done before though I'd heard about it, usually out on the plains. It meant concentrating on one group: the leaders if you could pick leaders out of that mess. We had to crowd them: no guns, that'd only make it worse. But we used ropes and boots and blistering curses, forcing them along parallel to the now leaning fences. Once moving, the pace increased and the other dumb cows followed, jostling to get in *behind* the lead group when they could've simply made their own direction. But some instinct made them follow and that was what Toohey wanted. With the lead group moving faster now, the tail end of the mass began to drag out and away and you could see the beginnings of a circle – with a gap – forming.

Then our riders moved in in a block, yelling louder, slashing with ropes, driving them to new terror. The gap closed and pretty soon the leaders had caught up with the tailers and then there was a jumble and a lot of bawling and some cows went down and would stay there, or have to be shot afterwards, but in a surpisingly short time they had come to a standstill under a roiling, choking dust cloud, bawling like demons from Hell.

'They call it a millwheel,' Toohey panted, as the cows bawled and crushed against each other. 'Friend described it to me once. You have to be prepared to lose a coupla dozen, mebbe more, but it'll stop 'em – and with our fences still holdin', we were lucky.'

It almost went wrong, though. One of the nighthawks thought he spotted a rider beyond the smoking brush and automatically took a couple of shots at him. The mass of cattle almost broke again, but we managed to control them and the rider sheepishly put his gun away.

We could find no tracks come daylight, but there was a broken bottle that had once held coal oil. No way of pinning the fire on anyone, of course. I was itching to brace Skip Dexter but we had to castrate some of the wilder steers or we would have more troubles than you could shake a stick at along the trail.

It was bloody, exhausting work and Jonesy, from Bob Barry's Double-B, lost some teeth when a wild hoof caught him in the mouth. Tiny Patterson had his nose broke and we all had our feet stomped on – and the coyotes and crows and buzzards had a banquet so rich half of them couldn't get off the ground, they had been such gluttons.

Then the branding started and it was a slice of hell, choking dust, smoke burning our throats, fighting the mavericks, falling into our blanket rolls at sundown and not even worrying if we never woke up come morning – then it started all over again. The preparation seemed endless, as if we would never move away from the Panhandle. Lieutenant Clegg was Wingfield's choice to ride with us and keep tabs on the head count and he was growing as restless and anxious as we were as the deadline to get the herd out of Pumicestone County drew closer by the hour.

Finally, one red dawn, we all gathered on the caprock, wagons on the slopes, teams in harness, riders with guns loaded, hats jammed down tight over their eyes, horses snorting and already anticipating the bite of spur rowels, the wranglers holding the remuda poised. I rode out to the head of the surprisingly docile herd, stood in the stirrups, lifted my hat and waved it in a northerly direction, yelling,

'All right – move 'em out! It's time to go to Colorado!'

A couple of dozen dust-clogged throats managed a cheer and a few rebel yells and then we took the first steps of the thousand-mile journey.

A rumble like a summer storm gathering trembled

the earth, but there were surprisingly few bellows and only a brief clash of horns and head tossing, but within minutes the ranch house and buildings disappeared behind a thick pall of dust.

If the Old Man was watching from the porch I didn't see him. The old so-and-so hadn't even wished me luck.

But Denny had, and so had Eleanor Chapman. And she'd sounded as if she meant it. *What the hell was that woman up to?*

But I had other things than that to occupy my mind – and for the next couple of months at least.

Because of delays, it was not only a race to clear the county line before the deadline, but if we didn't make good time, we'd be heading into cold weather with storms and heavy rains coming down from the north.

Not the best of conditions for a bunch of mostly amateur trail drivers, and a couple of thousand wild-eyed longhorns that only did what we wanted for as long as they felt like it. Then even experienced trail riders had their hands full. I tried not to think about how we'd handle it.

# CHAPTER 9

# TRAIL BOSS

West – we had to drive west before turning north. It was fifty miles to the New Mexico line and we would have to cross the Canadian before turning north and picking up the Goodnight-Loving trail. With luck a hundred miles would take us to the territory line and across the Cimarron into Colorado.

After that it was a long ways north to a hopeful market waiting in Pueblo. No one had been able to give me an accurate timetable for the beef trains so it would be hit-and-miss: we could arrive with the train already there or due in a day or two, or we could just miss it and have to wait another fortnight or even a month before its return.

A month's rest for the cattle on good graze would be fine, but the dealers would move in before they put on too much weight, and do their best to keep the price down.

So it was all a gamble – and just getting there was a damn big part of the odds we had against us.

Nature held a big stake in our success or failure: weather could swing one way or t'other and there wasn't a blamed thing we could do about that.The cattle couldn't be dismissed, either: the temperament of a few of the leaders actually decided just how well the drive would go, not just week by week, but day by day, even hour by hour.

These damn longhorns were a law unto themselves and we simply had to bite the bullet.

Rustlers might not be such a problem as a man might at first think: ours was a big herd and, no doubt while tempting to waiting wide-loopers, the size of our crew would likely give them pause to think twice. It was by no means certain, of course, and my orders were to give warning at the first sighting of *any* rider not with us, white man, red man or any other colour you like to name. I didn't aim to take any chances.

I was feeling my responsibilities, likely more than I needed to, but this was virtually my first big drive, surely so as a trail boss, and a lot of people's futures were riding on my shoulders. I didn't want to sound – or act – too pompous, but it was a fact, and many a man I'd shared tobacco and coffee with backed off, a mite puzzled, at some of my curtness or show of temper.

I tried to make it up but fact was there was a gap, slowly but surely, growing between the crew and myself. I'd read about the same sort of thing happening between a captain of a ship and his crew that he may have caroused with ashore, then became the Devil's Deputy once back at sea.

These thoughts bothered me and with all the other things to think about my day did not end at sundown and the finding of water for the herd. I did not sleep well, which, in turn, made me crotchety the next day.

Then it started all over again come next sundown.

But we battled our way to the New Mexico line, fought the Canadian's current. I had been lucky enough to find the crossing place very close to the ford the Old Man had told me about. Just as well, for several steers that wandered no more than a few yards from the main line were floundering within moments and washed away in seconds.

We lost sixteen on that first crossing and I saw the hard, worried looks of the men who had cows amongst the drowned ones. I could almost read their thoughts:

*Not fifty miles from home and we're losing cows on a quiet river crossing, and we've still got 1,000 miles to go! Some trail boss!*

You couldn't blame them for not having much faith in me.

Adam Clegg, dressed in civilian working clothes now, his uniform no doubt carefully folded and stowed in his warbag, rode alongside, looking at me sidelong from under the stiff brim of his new hat.

'I've seen enough rivers to know that wasn't anywhere near flooded, Stretch,' he said, carefully critical.

I knew what he was saying and felt myself go rigid in the saddle, but I held back from snapping: he had a right to criticize.

'I'm as big an amateur as the rest of you, Adam. I make no claims otherwise. I've done little trail driving, some during the war for the army, but there ain't many experts around to teach greenhorns the ropes.'

He frowned slightly then nodded as if he had just been told something he hadn't thought through. 'Yeah, I guess that's true. Let's hope we all get a chance along the way to get some real experience that'll stand by us if we run into extremes.'

I knew what he meant by 'extremes' and smiled wryly at his diplomacy. 'If it's as simple as rustlers or Indians we've already got plenty of experience between us – almost everyone here was in the war. But if there're other problems, like stampedes, floods or prairie fires. . . .' I shrugged. 'We learn as we go. All of us.'

He nodded, mouth grim. 'Yeah, and God help us, huh? Well, I'm not a religious man, not after seeing what war does to men, but I don't mind putting some faith in a talisman – or signs agin the evil eye.' He touched a musket ball slung on a thong around his neck. 'Had my name on it – a Johnny Reb's rifle muzzle was no more than a foot from my head, but it misfired. I almost died of a heart attack, mind, before I got the upper hand . . . and, of course, there's always' – he held up his right hand with middle and index fingers crossed, grinning.

I grinned back and waved him off to his post on drag with Bucky and Curly. Crossed fingers, making the sign of the cross, spitting into the wind or bowing to the sun at the moment of dawning – none of those things would make any difference when the first big trouble hit us.

And it came out of a red sundown even before we

reached the Cimarron.

A dozen riders, black against the fiery sky, thundering out of the deep shadows cast by low hills as the herd shambled on to a cramped plain of brownish grass. They timed it just right – as far as they were concerned.

The cattle were tired, eager to graze, already vexed and out of humour after a long, hot, dry day's drive. They were starting to spread out, heads down, some lowing, others snorting, a few rattling horns warningly. And they were in no mood to be disturbed as they began to relax and search for some grass with juice in it.

But these riders came a'whooping in, loosing several arrows, finding marks in dusty hides and spreading the panic. Rifle shots hammered and clattered, punching flame-daggered holes in the closing dusk, a few balls raising dust among the churning legs, snapping one or two.

That was all it needed: three cows went down with bullet-busted legs, bawling and thrashing, and the rest weren't about to stick around to see what was the cause.

With a concerted grunting bellow, the herd took off across the plains, trampling bedrolls already spread, forcing the cook to jump for his life, losing his big pot of newly peeled vegetables for the night's supper – *Sonofabitch Stew*, a favourite receipe of just about every darn trail cook I've ever known in the years that followed this night.

By the time he had run out of curses and stopped kicking his pots and pans, the herd was disappearing into the gathering darkness – and us with it in hot pursuit.

The raiders had spread out, obviously knew this area well, skirted the drag, shooting a few wild shots at our riders, and then turned in to the far side of the herd. It was in full stampede now, though there didn't seem to be much danger: the flats appeared to give a good run to the next line of hills and I was hoping that the worst that could happen would be that the steers would only shed a pound or two.

Apart from what the Indians might cut out.

I had the Henry to my shoulder, managed to pick out a rider against the dark background now, led him and fired. I brought down his horse and he flew over the animal's head, rolling and skidding. Somehow his pards managed to dodge him and he staggered to his feet, bringing up his rifle. Even as I triggered again and saw the bullet smack him off his feet, I noted it was short-barrelled, thick at the breech like a Spencer repeater, not the usual old muzzle-loader trade rifle.

That sounded warning bells, but I didn't have time to follow it through. The first of the steers went down and the way they spun and somersaulted and fell, I knew the appearance of the flats was misleading.

There were unseen potholes or gopher holes.

Two more steers crashed and I saw one Indian half stand in his wooden stirrups, draw his flatbow and slam an arrow home into the skidding cow. He was the only one I saw attempt to kill a steer – and I'd been thinking, naturally enough, that this was merely a raid for free meat.

Stampede the herd so as to keep us trail hands

busy, and while we were chasing our cows, they would drop a couple from the drag, dismount, hack off a haunch or a tongue, maybe some brisket, and then disappear back into the shadowed hills before we had the herd under control.

But their guns were still hammering – and I saw one of our riders fall from the saddle, another clutch at his shoulder as he dropped his rifle, sway drunkenly, fighting to stay mounted.

At the same time, I saw three of the raiders, angling into a wedge of the herd, isolating a dozen steers, concentrating on cutting them out. They were experts, did it in seconds and had the cows heading back towards the black hills before I got off three fast shots.

All of them missed. Shooting from a racing mount that was instinctively dodging gopher holes – thank God! – isn't much good for accuracy.

Clegg and Toohey and the others were scattered, dividing their attention between trying to turn the steers in on themselves so as to slow them, and dodging lead from the raiders. These *hombres* wanted to kill us as well as steal our cattle, it seemed.

I shouted and signalled to let the herd run but the remaining light was fading fast now, like someone lowering a giant blind. The rumble and bawling of the herd hadn't diminished and I couldn't tell if they had increased speed or not.

I wrenched the claybank's head around, angled back towards the drag. Something *burrrppped!* past my face and I knew I'd come close to getting my head shot off. I stretched out along the claybank's back, part of the mane whipping across my eyes. I glimpsed a rider, fired the Henry one-handed and almost lost it as it bucked. Not that it had a heavy recoil but I didn't have a firm grip and I tightened instinctively. I didn't want to lose my best weapon. Gripping with my knees, I reached across my body and got the Colt pistol out of the holster, saw a blurring shape coming, one hand raised, and fired right under my own face.

Burning powder grains stung my cheeks and I instinctively slammed my eyes shut, though I still saw the flash through the lids. My ears rang so loud I lost the sound of the stampede's thunder. When I opened my eyes, my vision was blurred but I glimpsed the raider, swaying in his saddle, a hand clawed into his chest. This time I made sure the Colt was clear of my face before I thumbed the hammer and fired. He jerked but didn't fall and then I lost him in the darkness. Cursing, I almost spilled from the saddle as the claybank swerved to miss a slashing horn.

Wheeling, juggling my guns, I holstered the Colt and levered another shell into the Henry's breech. But I'd fallen behind the main stampede now and seemed to be alone. Then I glimpsed the man I had wounded.

He was hunched over in the saddle, desperately hanging on, making for the line of brush at the edge of the hills. It was at least a half-mile off and I didn't figure he would make it.

He didn't. He toppled off and lay there, the horse running on only a few yards before pausing and looking around, just standing there, watching me approach.

The herd seemed to be slowing in the distance now. Gunfire was spasmodic. I figured the crew had things under control enough for me to take a look at this feller I'd downed.

There had been something strange about the way he handled his gun, his appearance in general, though I hadn't been able to pick out much detail in the poor light.

I dismounted warily a few yards from his sprawled body and even in the dark I saw why he had looked different from the other raiders.

He was a white man, still in range clothes except for a hat. He wore a cloth headband with a feather sticking up from the rear. In the dark, just a glimpse would be enough to mistake him for one of the Indian raiders.

Then I began to wonder just how many had been genuine Indians. . . .

The raiders disappeared into the night and the herd ran themselves out. I knew they would be scattered to hell and gone and we'd lose time rounding them up. As far as we could tell there were about a dozen downed but there could be more on the fringes that we were unable to find right now.

We had four men wounded, only one seriously.

I doubled-up nighthawk patrols and they spent a few complaining hours in the saddle. Then they were relieved by another shift, including myself. Good old Cookie, swearing a blue streak and forever damning himself by cursing the Almighty for allowing it all to happen to *him*, had nonetheless got us some hot grub and with gallons of his six-shooter coffee steaming away in his battered pots, we managed to come awake enough to sit our saddles.

At first light I singled out Clegg and we rode around the now more-or-less settled herd, though it was still scattered far and wide. Most were grazing, some were sleeping, other cows were literally licking their wounds. Four more had to be shot because of injuries, mostly broken legs, though one was badly gored.

'The damn tally book's gonna have more in the *Loss* columns than the *Profits*,' I growled.

'Kind of far from the Indian territory for this kind of raid,' Clegg allowed. 'You'd think they'd hit the others making due north, instead of riding all the way west after us.'

'Still plenty of maverick Kiowas hereabouts, but mighty few trail herds, Adam. Found an arrow in a downed steer – and one of them had snuck back and hacked a damn big haunch off it during the night. Arrow was a hunting shaft.'

'How d'you know that?'

'Twist on the fletching, the feathers – gives the arrow spin so it'll penetrate deeper – like into a buffalo, and drop him in his tracks.'

Clegg nodded. 'Then it seems it was a genuine Indian beef raid.'

I had been looking for the man I had downed, standing in the stirrups now. I saw his huddled shape way back here behind the herd. There was no sign of his mount but it could have gone on to the brush in the foothills.

'Come here and I'll show you something.'

Clegg saw he was a white man before we had reached the body. He dismounted swiftly, knelt and examined the face.

'Skin's been darkened with some sort of dye – probably the juice of some wild vegetable. But he was too lazy to strip to the waist, kept his white-man shirt on.'

I knelt beside him, pushed the dirt and blood-clogged hair back from the gravel-scarred face. 'I've seen him somewhere.'

Clegg snapped his head around. 'You know him then?'

I shook my head. 'Just recall his face. Dunno where I've seen him, but wasn't all that long back so likely was around Amarillo.'

'Then he'd know about the trail drive. . . .'

I nodded. 'Got a few renegade bucks together with some of his pards and tried his luck. . . .'

Clegg was still frowning. 'Still say it's a long way to come before doing that.'

'Ye-ah. . . .' I was studying the foothills. Two Indians, apart from the one I'd seen shoot an arrow into a steer, had been wounded but they'd got away. No one else had seen anyone they would have claimed as a white man, but those guns. . . .

We rode around and I found the downed Indian, a Kiowa all right, and his rifle was off to one side.It had been trampled in the stampede, the butt splintered. It was a Spencer carbine as I'd thought.

'Not many of these traded to renegade bucks,' Clegg said. 'Guns are in short supply, and if a man's lucky enough to find himself a repeater he hangs on to it. This could've been a bribe, to get the Indians to make the raid.'

That's the way I was thinking, too.

'Adam, I'm going into the foothills.'

He stiffened. 'Not alone!'

'Can't afford to take any of the men away – round-ing-up this herd is gonna lose us time.'

'If those raiders went in there, and they must've, you could get yourself killed.'

My nod was kind of absent because I was thinking ahead of the present. Aloud, I said, 'Some of the cows have been driven off – only a half-dozen or so, but they'll have left a trail I can follow. I'll take it easy.'

'What the hell can you do if you catch up with them? There'll be at least eight or nine – they didn't lose many.'

'No, but if I'm right, they'll have split with the Indians. They're finished with them now and the Kiowas'll be content with their free beef – and maybe a couple of guns the white renegades let them keep.'

Clegg was silent for a time. 'Even if you're right, there'll be four or five, and they'll kill you soon as they see you.'

I knew it was dangerous, but I had only one expla-nation for taking the chance. I hesitated, didn't want to sound too puffed-up with self-importance, but in the end, I told him, briefly, and hoped he would savvy,

'I'm the trail boss, Adam.'

He nodded slowly, eyes stalking my dirty face. 'So that makes it your responsibility. I've been hearing for years that you Southerners take your live-by codes seriously.' He thrust out his right hand. 'Lots of luck, Stretch.'

We gripped firmly and I had a strange, warm feel-ing that something decent had just happened here between us.

An *understanding* between old enemies.

# CHAPTER 10

# HEAVEN IN SIGHT

I smelled the smoke, tangy with a strong tincture of scorched meat.

It was cool in the timber although there wasn't much breeze, but this helped keep the smoke down amongst the vegetation. Rifle in hand, afoot, I moved in closer to where my nose told me the smell originated. It was past noon and what sunlight penetrated dappled the ground, but I no longer needed to search for tracks.

I found the Indians. Five of them, all with bloated bellies, sprawled in untidy postures around a burned-down fire that still had a hunk of Flag beef stuck on the end of a sharpened stick, charring in the coals. There were gobbets of fat and discarded stringy bits of meat scattered around, black with ants, and the buzzing of flies almost but not quite blotted out the sounds of their snores. What was left of the butchered cow was at the edge of the bush, looking disgusting and bloody with its spilled innards and white ribs.

It was typical. Just like Apaches, to which the Kiowa are related in some complicated way, once they had meat they couldn't go far without sampling it. One bite of the barely seared beef smashed down all barriers of restraint and they settled in for an orgy of gluttony. I remembered the Old Man telling me once how three Apache had stolen some Flag horses and he'd found them, in a stupor from having spent two days stuffing themselves with meat until they had consumed a whole damn horse between them.

He'd shot them where they lay with the big Dragoon .44 pistol he carried at that time. He'd been a tough old galoot in those pioneering days. You had to be to survive.

But I had no intention of shooting these beauties. I tried waking them, shaking their shoulders first, booting them lightly in the ribs, then a little harder, all without result. They snored on, belched and broke wind in their stupor. I saw the smashed stone whiskey jug then: seemed the white renegades had supplied them with firewater, too. They must have had a truly memorable orgy.

But I needed some information and I grabbed a glowing stick from the coals of the camp-fire, pressed it against the foot of one of the Kiowa. That got results although his eyes were glazed as he rubbed his foot vigorously, still sluggish and torpid. As he finally sat up, he fell sideways, then sat again, backing away from my rifle muzzle that I waved in front of his face.

I'd picked up a bit of Indian lingo when playing with some of the reservation kids while growing up on Flag. I remembered some now, grunted a couple of questions at him. He shook his head, either not understanding or too dopey yet to reply.There was an ounce of whiskey left in the broken bottom of the stone jug and I handed it to him.

He focused on that all right, grabbed with trembling hands, spilled most of it but apparently got some down his throat the way he coughed and hawked. He blew his nose on his fingers and wiped them on the grass, staring at me with reddened, watery eyes.

*Who were the white men. . . ?* That was my question and I must've repeated it a dozen times before he made some kind of a reply. It was little more than a series of grunts, but I pressed the rifle muzzle into his groin and his eyelids flew wide, his fingers twisting into the grass. He shook his head quickly and I asked one more time as I cocked the Henry's hammer. It finally got through to him.

He only knew them as outlaws who lived in the territory and peddled whiskey and the occasional gun to the Indians. For a promise of these things and all the beef they could carry away, he and his companions had agreed to make the raid on our trail herd.

'Give me a name.' I kept insisting and finally he said gutturally, 'Dun-ka.'

I repeated the name slowly and he nodded, easing his hips so as to get some of the pressure off his groin.

'I want white-man name!' I snapped.

'Dun-ka, Dun-ka!' he said emphatically, sweat beading his now sallow face. I heard his bulging belly rumble with its overload of half-raw beef, and moved to one side in case he suddenly threw up. 'Dun-ka!' Then his face brightened and he added, 'Bor! *Bor*!' Nodding for emphasis, even trying a smile.

*Dun-ka Bor? Still sounded like an Indian name to me.*

Then, running them together in my mind, I suddenly got it: Indians have some trouble with our syllables and vowels at times and, remembering the man with the vaguely familiar face I'd shot during the stampede I came up with, 'Duncan Borg?'

He was nodding like his head would break loose from his neck now. 'Dun-ka Bor!' He said it over and over until I had to tell him to shut up.

I stood slowly and decided to leave him and his snoring pards where they were. I didn't know where the rest of my cows were, but that didn't matter so much at the moment – especially when two white men appeared out of the brush, guns in their hands. The one with the long, dirty-looking blond hair held a sixgun, but his sidekick, squat and beard-shagged with eyes like a snake's, held a Spencer carbine.

'So you had to come lookin', McQuade,' said the blond one. He glanced at the squat man. 'Just as well we come back to settle these big brave warriors when we did, Jesse.'

'Settle McQuade, too,' Jesse growled and looked mighty eager. 'Best drop that Henry, McQuade.'

I still had the hammer cocked from when I'd been bothering the Indian who now sat there looking from the newcomers to me, wondering what was happening. My rifle was pointing in the general direction of the white men who still had traces of dye on their faces and hands. I knew they'd been with the raiders last night and from what the blond one had said, they had come back to finish off the surviving Indians. By now, they'd likely killed any of their companions who'd made it clear . . . dead men can't talk.

'*Down*, I said!' Jesse snapped, bringing up the Spencer, only now starting to cock the big mule-ear hammer.

He never made it. I used a wrist action to tilt the barrel up as I fired. It rose naturally, then very fast when the rimfire cartridge exploded. Jesse grunted as he stumbled back three or four paces, dropping the Spencer, his thick legs starting to buckle.

But I saw all that only peripherally. As soon as I'd fired, I tossed the smoking Henry towards the blond man and he jumped back, as he brought up his sixgun, firing wild. By then I had my Colt out of the holster, went down to one knee and put two bullets into him. He turned around and did a kind of quick-step before twisting even further and falling on his back. His heels drummed briefly but he didn't move after that.

Jesse was moaning and rolling about, clawing at his thick chest. The Indian I'd questioned had gone very still, his cheeks blowing in and out and suddenly he spun aside and threw up violently. His companions continued to snore on. I left him heaving and knelt beside Jesse who looked up at me with wide, knowing eyes. It was probably the widest they had ever opened. There was blood on his thick underlip.

I picked up the Henry, now thumbed back the hammer and let the barrel kind of wander in the direction of his face. 'Is he Duncan Borg?' I jerked my head towards the blond.

Watching my trigger finger, Jesse shook his head.

'You're not – so where is he?'

He worked his mouth, coughed wetly as he tried to answer. 'Got – shot – last night. . . .'

*Must've been the one I'd nailed.*

I knew the name Duncan Borg, knew it as being that of an outlaw who ran with a small wild bunch in the Indian territory. Another memory stirred, way back, that somehow combined the name with that of Dexter, maybe not Skip, but possibly Bruiser, the older one.

Jesse didn't have long. I nudged him not too gently. 'Skip Dexter put you up to this?' He just stared and I prodded him again. He winced, breath coming hard and wheezing now.

He nodded. 'Said to hassle you far as we . . . could – bust-up your herd – wear you down to a frazzle.'

'You fixing to try again? The rest of you that got away last night?'

His head rolled sort of limply and blood was trickling from a corner of his mouth now. 'They gone back to – territory. Never 'spected you . . . put up . . . so much fight. . . .'

I smiled grimly. 'All ex-soldiers, Jesse. But Skip wouldn't have the brains to figure that side of it. All he'd see was that we were greenhorns on a long trail drive. . . .'

111

But I was talking to myself now: Jesse had gone.

And five minutes later so had I.

The Indian who had been sick had crawled to a hunk of fly-ridden beef lying in the dirt and was trying to hack a slice from it without cutting off a finger when I moved back into the brush to where I'd left the claybank.

Talk about a glutton for punishment.

Clegg and Toohey met me halfway back to the herd and Toohey volunteered to go bury the dead men and bring back the rest of the cows – there would be only three or four, and the Indians wouldn't give him any trouble.

'So Skip Dexter can't let it go,' Adam Clegg said, as we rode back to the herd. 'He aims to settle with you, one way or another, I think, Stretch.'

'Always an unforgiving clan, the Dexters.'

There must have been something in the way I said it because he gave me a sharp look. 'Something else?'

I didn't answer at first. 'I dunno, Adam. Skip and me didn't ever get along, but that could be said of Skip and almost everyone in Pumicestone County. Old Man Dexter was half-crazy, made his own moonshine, poisoned himself and others with it a couple times. He ended up partially paralyzed after a wagon accident, which is maybe why Skip never went to war, though his brother did. He was the one they called Bruiser. They had a small but good section northwest of Flag, but the Dexters didn't work it much, let it go – a waste, Pa always said. I never went up that way after I came back but I was just wondering. . . .' I

112

paused, still not sure. 'The Old Man snapped up some smaller places cheap when folk went bust while the war was on. Just wondering if Dexter's Cross D was one of 'em.'

'Would explain Skip keeping after you.'

'And busting the Old Man's legs. But adds to the puzzle as to why Pa accepted him as a horse-breaker on Flag. He'd know Skip always held a grudge.'

Clegg had no answer to that. Nor did I. And I had a sudden impatience to get this herd to market and return to Flag.There was only Denny and a couple of local cowhands there now. And the Chapman woman, of course. If Skip wanted to make a move against Flag there would never be a better time for him to try.

'You ever know that Captain Chapman? Husband of Eleanor?' I asked suddenly. 'She says he was killed at Second Manassis.'

Clegg shook his head. 'Never there myself and I don't recall him. Met a Major Chapman briefly on Ulysses' staff, but he was a career man and is still alive, got a wife and seven or eight kids back in Pennsylvania.'

I let it go. The herd was in sight now and we increased our speed as we closed with it.

By this time we were heading due north and that night Bob Barry gave me more problems. He came to sit with me just after supper while I was trying to get the tally books in order by the light of an oil lamp standing on an upended crate behind the chuck-wagon.

'Got a minute, Stretch. . . ?'

I knew by his tone something I wasn't going to like was coming. His face told me he didn't much care for whatever it was, either, or maybe it was just having to approach me about it, knowing whatever it was would upset me.

He was right. What Bob wanted to do was take his hundred or so head of Double B steers and cut away from the herd, go west and sell them to the army at Fort Bascom.

'I got an ailin' wife back at my spread, you know that, Stretch. I need money now. I – I'll likely sell-up for what I can get there and with the money I can take her some place where she can get proper treatment.'

I savvied his predicament, but it was a goddamn nuisance: we had over 2,000 head and we had to cut out roughly a hundred wearing the Double B brand.

'It's gonna take time to cut your herd out, Bob, and we're behind schedule. Besides, the army won't give you forty bucks a head like you can expect at Pueblo.'

'Yeah, well, that's it, Stretch,' he said slowly, scratching at his tufts of grey hair hanging over his right ear. 'You "expect" that forty bucks – but mebbe you won't get it, neither.'

'Get more than the four a steer's worth down in Texas. Charlie Goodnight and Ollie Loving aren't fools, Bob. They've made a couple of drives up this way. It paid off each time. They're riding high.'

He nodded vigorously, face twisted in indecision. 'It's all I can think of, Stretch! I know you or the other fellers can't buy me out. Drifter came through yest'y while you were away. He said Fort Bascom's hungry for beef.'

'Chancy, Bob. A drifter's word. . . .'

Suddenly he looked decisive, mouth tight. 'Nope! I'm gonna do it. I – I *gotta*, Stretch! Amy's all I got. She never got over losin' the boy in the war . . . we been together nigh on forty years. I – I owe it to her to give her the best chance I can.'

I understood his dilemma and there was a chance the drifter had been right, I suppose: I couldn't refuse.


By late afternoon of the next day, Bob had his small herd together. He'd lost eleven on the drive so far but he made no complaint about that and I told him there'd be no account for his share of the grub or trail plant. He was a proud man and didn't want charity, but I talked him round in the end and next morning he started his herd moving west with his two cowhands.

That left us three men short and that meant we had a tougher drive ahead of us than the one we'd had so far.

But right after breakfast, I hazed the crew back into their saddles, some still trying to swallow Cookie's leathery flapjacks, and yelled, 'We're moving out! All points north to Pueblo – the non-stop Texas Express! Now, let 'em roll!'


We 'rolled' for three days, up on to the Staked Plains, after negotiating the Caprock Escarpment with nothing more than minor troubles and delays. The coun-

115

try was easy going, dry, flat tablelands, but the grass was long enough to satisfy the ever-hungry longhorns once we bedded-down for the night, but not so enticing they wanted to stop during the day for more than a few mouthfuls.

Water was a priority as we approached the Cimarron and the herd had to go without for two days. But Toohey scouted on ahead once he was certain the herd was going to behave for the day and found enough waterholes to keep us going. It was dusty, choking work in hot, blasting winds.

The Cimarron Crossing was bothering me: you could never tell with these rivers until you were on top of them, just how the flow was going to be. The Cimarron was muddy which meant rains upstream somewhere, but the current wasn't excessive, though we still lost five cows and two horses. Actually, the Swede found the horses downstream later while chasing a couple of breakaways and they followed him back to the herd and remuda, so my worries about the crossing had been for nothing.

Then, north of the Santa Fe Trail cut-off, Capulin Mountain almost due north of us, I figured we must be close to the Colorado line. Raton Pass was about thirty, forty miles north-west and I decided to make for there.

Then Toohey came back from scouting for water with news that electrified the entire outfit.

'There's a town west of the mountain! Looks fairly new, not very big, an' only partly built, but they sure are friendly! Say that with a capital "F"!'

Toohey had ridden in and been met with smiles

and pats on the back – and there seemed to be a lot of handsome young women showing well-turned ankles and even stockingless legs up to the knees, giving welcoming smiles and promises of delights that would make a man think he was in heaven.

And that, indeed, was the name of the unexpected trail town – *Heaven's Gateway.*

Someone must have had a weird sense of humour. A more fitting name would have been *Hell's Doorway.*

We found *that* out the hard way.

# CHAPTER 11

# LET US PREY!

The men were restless just knowing there was an unexpected town – and women and booze – just over the next ridge.

I didn't feel too much excitement. I knew there would be trouble. Had to be when you turn loose a trail crew starved of both the things they talked about constantly and then have them suddenly appear within reach.

The herd felt it, too. They must have wondered what in hell had happened, the way they were hazed along like they never had been before on this drive. The cowboys were at their best, riding fast and precisely, knowing just what they wanted, delivering it at top speed. A potential breakaway would only just have to form the thought in its bovine brain and before the animal could make a move, there was a cowboy alongside, forcing it back into the mob with a hefty kick behind the ear. Two horses were gored, though not badly. I saw the second one – it was Bucky's – and I rode up and rammed my horse into his, almost unseating him. Startled, he fought the reins and the writhing mount which was bleeding from the gash on its chest. He looked at me with a mixture of anger and surprise.

'Jesus, boss! What the hell?'

'I like your fast reaction to a breakaway, Bucky, but not when it gores your horse! We don't have that big a remuda we can afford to have horses drop out while horn wounds mend.'

'Sorry, boss,' he said, surly.

'Quit worrying about that goddam town. Get the herd over the ridge and *then* we'll check it out. *Comprende?*'

He nodded, anger fading: a good man and he knew he was at fault. 'OK, Stretch. Bit too eager to get me a look at some lace and smell some bedroom perfume, I guess.'

I rode away, giving him a half-grin and a wave. Others had seen the incident and hopefully would benefit from it. I didn't want to have to start talking cuts to pay if they didn't behave or that kind of thing.

The ridge was steeper than it looked and the herd resisted the best efforts of the cowboys to drive it faster.

But by late afternoon we'd made the crest and as the cows flowed over the top in a bawling, brown-and-white stream, we saw the town – or what there was of it.

It was set in a small basin that was well-grassed and watered.There were a couple of dozen buildings, raw pine timber bright yellow against the green of the grass, some peeled logs white as bone. There wasn't much plan to the lay-out, the buildings kind of scattered as if folk built wherever they wanted.

Somehow that made me a mite uneasy. I just had a feeling that it meant the place wasn't intended to be permanent. But who would build a temporary town way out here? Unless the Goodnight-Loving Trail was going to be used a lot more than it was at present. Then it would be first in, first served – and a small town with all the pleasures a cowboy held dear available could make a quick fortune.

And that, to me, meant exploitation of trail crews.

But the men were ready to ride in and paint the place red, or tear it down in their exuberance, whichever offered the most entertainment. The herd was moving of its own accord, now, heading for the sweet-smelling grass on flats outside the town. I noticed some rail fencing then as if the townsfolk were building holding pens. *I could be wrong about the place being only temporary.*

Then there was a cheer and a slew of rebel yells and hats flying into the air and I hipped quickly in saddle.

A painted buckboard that had had a fringed surry-like top added, was coming quickly from out amongst the buildings, overloaded with waving, laughing women in crinoline and gingham, all colourful. A couple of pink and green umbrellas, waved, too, and thin female voices – the first we had heard in weeks – drifted up.

'Howdy, there, cowboy! Welcome to Heaven's Gateway!'

'C'mon on down and sample what we've got – and what the bar's got, too!'

'First-class likker! First-class gals!'

'Oh, lordy, I got a feelin' I ain't gonna be restful – nor lonely – tonight!'

'Full moon, too, boys! And you know what that means!' A pale blonde gave a drawn-out wolf howl, received due applause. '*Anything goes!*'

And so on, a lot of it drowned out by the ribald shouts of the crew. Adam Clegg rode up, smiling crookedly.

'Wish I'd brought my troop along so's you could control 'em, Stretch?'

'But would you be able to control your troop?' I countered and he laughed.

'Gonna be a wild night, I guess.'

The cowpokes were gathered around the buckboard now, some leaning from saddles and giving or getting kisses and hugs from the women. Close-up you could see they were second-hand goods, but they weren't as bad as some I'd seen by a long way. It wouldn't have mattered to the crew if they had been grandmothers. . . . I knew I was going to have my hands full this night.

There was a fat man in a grey suit driving the buckboard and when he brought out a stone jug of whiskey, ready to hand out free drinks, I spurred across, yelling.

'Put that jug away, mister!' He looked startled, then turned to the reaching hands of some of the cowboys, gave me a mocking smile and lifted the jug towards them.

I drew and fired. The jug shattered, liquor splashed and women squealed and the fat man cursed. 'The *hell're* you doin'?' he demanded. Then, trying to enlist the backing of the sober-faced crew, he added, 'Your boss ain't a Bible-banger by any chance. . . ?'

I waved the Colt's smoking barrel in the fat man's sweating face and he leaned far back in the driving seat. The ladies were watching very warily now.

'I need my men sober,' I said carefully. 'My first concern's the herd. We get that bedded down, nighthawks set, *then* the others are free to ride into town and you can dish out all the free liquor you want.' I locked a hard gaze with the fat man's. 'But I guess not much'll be free in that saloon I see, huh? Not after the first couple of rounds.'

'We-ell, was just a welcomin' gesture, friend,' he said, eyes narrowed, his smile without even a touch of warmth. 'We're all here to have a little fun and make a little profit. You're our first trail herd. Weren't expectin' any up this way for another month or two – only got the town half-built.'

'Half-built, but double the fun still available!' said one fiery-haired woman waving a green umbrella, looking at me with cool eyes, smiling with lips as red as blood. 'You come and look me up, trail boss. I'll bet I can take your mind off your herd!'

That brought plenty of laughter and I grinned. 'Bet you could, too.' I turned to the cowboys who were starting to climb into the buckboard, the women squealing and fighting them off feebly.

'Let's get the herd bedded-down, fellers!' I

bawled, earning some hard looks from the men, too. 'Then we'll sort out who's going where and when.'

They grumbled but calmed down pretty quickly, realizing only a couple of hours' more work separated them from the delights of Heaven's Gateway. . . .

It was simple enough in the end.

I split the crew into two lots, and they drew straws to see who would be the first on nighthawk duty. There was plenty of cursing and twice as much whooping and laughter. I got them settled down and said flatly, 'First lot work from supper till ten o'clock. The fat man says the town'll stay open as long as we want it to, all night if necessary. Second watch will come back at *ten o'clock sharp* to relieve the first lot of nighthawks. Anyone doesn't get relieved, he stays put till someone comes to take his place. *He does not go looking for his replacement no matter how late he is* – and he can settle his problems later, himself, without restriction.' I knew that would mean some knock-down-drag-out brawls, but I figured to lay-over for a few days to let the cattle get the benefit of plentiful grass and water, so it would work out. Besides, it was always best to let the men settle their own differences.

'This apply to you, boss?' asked someone from beyond the camp-fire: I think it was Curly.

'To everyone except Cookie. He can have his turn in town and then come back and see there's plenty of black coffee waiting – and he can patch up any broken heads there might be.'

They liked that: I guess they saw it as my OK for

them to get into as many fights as they wanted. I didn't mean it quite that way, of course, but it would be stupid not to admit there were bound to be brawls.

I just hoped they didn't wreck the town. . . .

Some townsmen volunteered to come watch the herd so *all* the crew could enjoy what was offered earlier and for longer. But I didn't want strangers riding nighthawk on the herd.

I declined, but when some of the townsfolk started to get huffy, I relented a little and said we could use an extra four or five hands, just to make sure the herd settled down and stayed that way.

It seemed to satisfy them and they drew straws to see which four townsmen would join the outfit temporarily.

The quartet was made up of tough-looking men in workclothes, looking fit and – it seemed to me – forcing their grins as the first nighthawks anticipated leaving the herd early for town.

'The change-over stays as-is – relief at ten o'clock, not before, and hopefully, not much after.'

It was all settled eventually and I hazed them into seeing the herd bedded-down properly. Then they all ran for the creek, stripped and scrubbed with sand – me, too – and then lined-up for advance money. I didn't have much travelling cash and I rode into town with the first bunch – they reached town a good five minutes before me, in their eagerness – and I went looking for the fat man, found him just inside the almost completed saloon. Two walls were canvas as was part of the roof and the bar was no more than a plank resting on a couple of kegs, but my crew were served quickly by a broken-nosed barkeep.

The fat man's name was Shell O'Connor and I saw there were a couple of card and dice tables set up in one corner as a swamper moved around lighting oil lamps.

'Hardly any free cash, O'Connor,' I told him. 'Can give you a chit with a limit on it for the men – if you'll trust me to settle-up on our way back from Pueblo.'

The idea seemed new to him, though Goodnight had told Pa it was common enough practice these days.

O'Connor gave it some thought. 'No offence, McQuade, but I don't know you. I guess I can trust most men but – how about this? You give me, say, a hundred head and that'll cover whatever kinda bill your crew run up.'

'A hundred! Hey, they're not here to finance the building of your town. I figure to get forty dollars a head in Pueblo. A hundred's too many to give you.'

'You'll likely get your forty; I hear they're droolin' for beefsteak. But you're still a long ways south of Pueblo, McQuade. Theoretically, I can run to maybe – seven bucks a head. . . ?'

That would be $700 for the crew to spend a couple of nights in this dump. And O'Connor would treble that in Pueblo. 'Thirty head.'

His eyes were like basalt and the smile was a hundred miles from being friendly. 'I sure hope all the trail bosses ain't as hard as you are, McQuade.'

'Deal or not?' I asked impatiently.'

He scrubbed a hand around his pink, flabby jowls.

The eyes were no softer, the smile no friendlier. 'Well, seein' as this is our first *almost*-official night, OK.'

He made no attempt to shake hands so I wrote out a bill of sale and signed it. 'You can collect your steers come morning.'

'All the same to you, I'll have my men who're helpin' yours' – he paused a little for that to sink in – 'bring 'em back when they come in tonight.'

'No. You'll disturb the herd. They'll be jumpy enough after the drive. I want 'em to settle down. You'll get your cows come morning.'

We left it at that and I watched for a while, fending off a couple of the women. To make it clear, I'm not averse to women and I've met and had my share of soiled doves over the years, but I picked up something harder and more calculating in the experienced eyes of these gals, even the younger ones. Some looked kind of vicious.

A couple made insulting remarks and I guess I was expected to react to 'em: a couple of bouncers with sawn-off axe handles were standing by. I ignored them with a twisted smile and then one young gal, about twenty, but already showing signs of wear and tear, brought me a drink.

I don't like whiskey much on its own: I'd been gutshot in Georgia and my belly wasn't as cast-iron as it used to be.

She said, 'This'll get your interest, Mr Trail Boss,' – a stringy blonde with too much make-up and I could see her bodice was grimy. New or not, Heaven's Gateway was no more than just another trail town whose sole existence was to empty the

126

pockets of trail drivers as quickly and effortlessly as possible. Their motto could've been *Let us prey!*

'I need some water with it.'

Her thin, arched eyebrows lifted and she shook her head slowly, called loudly to the 'keep, 'Mungo, our trail boss wants water to mix with his redeye! It's too strong for him!'

That got some laughter and strange looks – which was what she had intended – but I was given a small glass jug of slightly cloudy water. I topped up the whiskey and sipped. The fact that I didn't toss it down brought more behind-the-hand remarks mostly from the saloon gals and the townsmen. My crew knew about my old wound and how I preferred beer to hard liquor but the barkeep seemed hostile about the diluted whiskey.

Still, he drew me a foaming glass of beer without comment and the young whore moved on to try her luck elsewhere. I called for another beer and I thought I saw the 'keep pour a shotglass of whiskey – or something – into it.

'I don't mix my drinks this early, feller,' I told him, and he wanted to give me an argument. My feeling that this night was all wrong somehow, despite the good time my crew seemed to be enjoying, was stronger than ever.

The 'keep gave me some lip and I grabbed his shirtfront, slammed him face first into the plank, then dragged him halfway across. Turning him on his back, I poured the beer into his mouth until he choked and spluttered.

The room was silent and I was glad to see three of

my crew had lined up beside me, ready for trouble. I frowned when I noticed the wrangler, Stew Shorter, lying on the floor.

'Thought Stew could hold his booze?'

Red was swaying near me and grinned owlishly. 'Cast-iron tank couldn't hold this stuff, boss. Kicks like a mule.'

The 'keep struggled free, slid back to his side of the bar and then came up swinging a bung-starter. I saw him out of the corner of my eye, whipped aside in time, grabbed his wrist, twisted the cane-handled mallet from his grip and hit him with it between the eyes. He dropped out of sight. I belted the mallet on the plank and all eyes turned to me.

'Boys, we'll call it a night. I'm sorry, but this is a big set-up. We're all gonna get fleeced if not worse.'

O'Connor came raging in, indignant. 'I resent that, McQuade!'

'Be my guest. Just don't try to stop us leaving.'

I was holding my cocked pistol by now and grabbed the bleary-eyed Red's arm, shook him. 'Get the men.'

'Aw, Stretch! We – we on'y just started! I – I ain't even been snuggled-up with a gal yet. . . .'

I put a shot into the roof, punching a hole in the stretched canvas. Men dived for cover. 'Break it up! *Now*!'

It wasn't that easy, even with my gun out. More townsmen came rushing into the bar, more than we'd seen around town earlier. *Where had they been hiding? And why?*

They held clubs and some had guns. My crew were

too drunk – or had they been slipped something in their whiskey?

The newcomers moved in, swinging clubs, one kicking the prone Stew on the floor. I shot him in the leg and other guns started banging. We hit the floor, and I tried to gather the men but it was chaos now, the women squealing and running to get out of the way. Stew was flung over Red's shoulder – he was sobering fast now the gunfire had started – and with the others stumbling, one man retching, we made for the door.

There was shooting outside in the street, the clatter of hoofs, men swearing, then Clegg and Jonesy came in, both bleeding from facial wounds, guns in hand.

'Stretch!' Adam yelled. 'C'mon, man! It's a trap! Those men they sent us were cutting-out cows soon as they got there, more came out of the brush. We've got two men wounded and the herd's ready to run!'

With back-up now, we raked the room with gunfire till our guns were empty, backing out. Somehow we got the crew into their saddles where instinct took over and they lifted the reins and rode in the direction we pointed their mounts.

Men spilled out of the saloon into the street shooting after us as we raced into the night back to the camp. I looked back – some were mounting, all had guns.

The camp was chaotic, the nighthawks, those still able to sit a horse anyway, were struggling to keep the milling, bawling cattle together.

The steers were on hair-trigger, ready to stampede.

'Hell! Must be twenty men comin'!' shouted some-one, pointing back towards the town.

'The bastards are after the herd!' Clegg growled, trying to reload his Remington pistol awkardly in the dark. He had a spare cylinder already primed with powder charge and lead balls but was fumbling at the release pin.

I got my own spare cylinder locked in the Colt's frame, and said, grimly, 'They want our cows? All right! Let's give 'em to the sons of bitches!'

I rode into the herd firing into the ground under the feet of the closest steers. It was enough to set them off, bawling and snorting. Clegg and the others spread out, guns stabbing flame, and suddenly the herd was off, running in unstoppable stampede. We hazed them mercilessly.

Over the flats, smashing down the partly built rail fences, heading straight for the band of men coming from the town. The riders hauled rein, unable to believe their eyes as they saw all those curving horns jiggling and catching the starlight as the herd bore down upon them. Panicked, they wheeled their mounts and started to race back towards town – or anywhere else as long as they stayed ahead of that thousand tons of terror thundering down upon them.

Our danders were well and truly aroused by now and we were almost as crazy as the maddened steers, because this had been a helltown in the making – being built with the sole purpose of preying on trail herds and their crews, dividing the spoils, stealing other men's cattle and selling them at the high prices being offered in Pueblo and Denver. Ready and willing to kill every last man in the trail crew.

So, we destroyed it.

The steers smashed down the partly built buldings, shredded the tent dwellings, rampaged through the twisted streets, the terrified populace fleeing before them. Some traded a few shots with us but their hearts weren't in it. We weren't out to cause a slaughter – just destruction. If some townsfolk were caught up in it – too bad!

What was left after the herd had battered its way through – splintered timbers, trampled canvas – we burned.

Come daylight, rounding up the herd again, the town ceased to exist. But Toohey found two steers in a half-demolished shed carrying the Double B brand. Cookie was tending one of the injured townsman under a tree. He looked at me wide-eyed as I approached. I guess I looked pretty damn scary, blackened, torn clothes, face bruised and scratched. I levered a shell into the Henry's breech, placed the muzzle against the man's knee. 'Where'd you get those Double B cows?'

He was yellow clear through. Told us straight-off how they had jumped Bob Barry and his men, killed them, aiming to add the cows to our herd after they drugged our crew and stole it.

'Good night's work, then,' opined Adam Clegg, a crude bandage around his head.

'Yeah,' I said with satisfaction. 'A damned good night's work.'

# CHAPTER 12

# POINTS NORTH

There was a lot of rounding-up to do, and near sundown the next day, with most of the cows herded together now – they tend to come drifting in where they see bunches of other cows: saved us some work – we found out what a miserable, greed-driven bunch of sonuvers had inhabited Heaven's Gateway.

Some of those men – and the odd woman! – waited in the shadows of the rock walls and the scattered patches of timber. When, wearily, I delegated a couple of men with myself, to watch the herd while the rest of the crew went for supper, those sidewinding snakes hit us.

It was designed as a nuisance raid, but if some of their lead found one or two of us, that'd be OK with them. They swept in silently and suddenly charged the settling herd from a few yards away, masked by the fast-closing night. A volley of shots, including the thunder of a shotgun and – no prizes for guessing! –

we had us a brand new stampede.

But they should have waited a few minutes longer, till the bone-aching crew had settled down to supper, boots off, belts slacked, mounts off-saddled. The raiders were a mite too impatient and started shooting just as the crew reached the chuckwagon and the makeshift camp.

With the other two nighthawks, I was returning the fire, racing to cut off bellowing, snorting steers before they got into a stampede stride. I threw up the Henry as I glimpsed a raider against a patch of glowing sky. He somersaulted over his mount's rump and was a writhing shadow last I saw of him as I swept on, triggered into the ground, turning aside a pair of wild-eyed Texas monsters.

Then the crew who'd gone for supper came back in a stampede of their own, tired, cranky, wild-eyed, both horses and men thundered in, guns blazing, out for blood. They were shooting across the heaving backs of the steers, finding human targets now. You don't play pat-a-cake with the likes of these killers. There was a good deal of lead flying around and a bullet lifted hair and a thin layer of hide from my claybank's rump. His rear end slewed and he whinnied and snorted and tried to bite my leg all at the same time. I was slammed this way and that, lost one stirrup, gripped the rifle tighter as I used my other hand to twist up a handful of flying mane. I managed to stay aboard but only just and the claybank figured he'd had enough abuse these past weeks, propped and skidded. I floundered like a greenhorn, tumbling off, though still hanging on to the mane, until the horse reared in fury and jerked me off my feet. When I hit the ground his forefeet came whistling down, the hoofs reaching for me, ready to cut me to pieces. I rolled desperately, still grasping the rifle.

A galaxy of lights swirled in front of my eyes and I realized I'd banged my head pretty damn hard on the ground. I tasted dust and grit, staggered up, and was just straightening when a horseman came charging down almost on top of me. I didn't hesitate, swung the rifle up and thrust the long barrel straight at the man who was throwing down with a sixgun. I triggered first and the shot literally blew him out of the saddle and I lunged sideways. Even so I was hit by a flying stirrup – it was that close.

By now the herd was gone and there was nothing we could do to stop it. The cows were mighty tired and likely wouldn't run all that far before slowing, straggling, finally coming to a halt – but scattered to hell-and-gone. The trail-town predators were satisfied, though they'd left a few men on the ground – and so had we. Jensen would be lucky to make it as far as Pueblo, and my best point rider, Chad Trevayne, had a broken ankle and Big Brady Toombes probably a collarbone according to Cookie, our resident medic – or as near as we had. The women seemed to have got away unscathed.

Clegg and Toohey were walking among the downed townsmen, kicking them to their feet, wounded or not, except for three who weren't moving for anyone, not this side of Hell. They dragged and shoved and cuffed two staggering men into the light of Cookie's fire. Both had wounds, one in the upper arm, and he moaned that the bone was broke, the other limping from a bullet that had lodged near his hip, and there was blood on his shirt-front. He coughed. Cookie glared.

'Someone tie them varmints up to a log – I ain't tendin' them till I get finished with our boys.' He spat in the direction of the hang-dog townsmen. 'An' mebbe I'll be too blamed tired to tend you at *all*.'

'My arm's broke!'

Cookie snatched at his ladle and brandished it at the townsman. 'Like to try for a broken jaw?'

The man fell into sullen silence. The limping one sat down heavily on a log, gasping, rubbing his hip wound, wheezing now. The firelight washed over his strained, dirt-smeared face. I stiffened. *It was a mass of twisted scars and burned-away flesh, completely without eyebrows, half an ear gone.* And when his hat fell off I saw that he had no hair at all, just a bald skull, this, too, writhing with scar tissue.

He saw me staring, turned his head away quickly, but not quite fast enough. Adam Clegg hissed an epithet beside my ear. 'God almighty! That . . . that's Colonel Lawton! He was in charge of the Reconstruction at Amarillo but he caused so much hell with the locals, Wingfield was sent in to court-martial him, but Lawton deserted, went bad. . . .'

'You might've known him as 'Lawton', Adam, but even those scars can't hide his looks from me. He was supposed to've been blown apart by Yankee shellfire at Monroe Station years ago, but seems he survived.' I leaned closer and those dead, almost lidless eyes stared bleakly into my face. 'You might've been lucky at Monroe, but your luck's run out now.' I turned to Clegg. 'Adam, meet Henry Dexter, otherwise known as Bruiser, esteemed and much-hated big brother of our old friend Skip – the bully of Amarillo.'

*I was only fourteen or so at the time. Pa had had a set of hand-tooled saddle-bags made by old Sebastiano, a local Mexican craftsman. I didn't know what he intended to do with them but they were mighty fine, had bucking broncos and spurs, cactus and distant mountains carved in relief.*

*I wasn't allowed to touch them, of course, but one time when Pa was out on round-up and I had to ride to school, I took them with me. By lunch time they'd disappeared from my old smoke gelding. I knew who'd taken 'em, of course: had to be Skip Dexter. And it was, so I gave him a hiding down behind the privy block, so bad he didn't dare return to class. But when I was riding home that afternoon, saddle-bags slung on the old smoke again, Skip reappeared – with big brother Bruiser, who was about twenty then.*

*The elder Dexter gave me one hell of a belting: I could hardly mount the old smoke. Strangely, they left the saddle-bags and when I finally dragged my tail back home, I was relieved to find Pa was still out on the range and would be camping there for a couple of days.*

*But Willard, my older brother, was there. I told him what had happened and he rode out, grim-faced, sixgun rammed in his belt. . . . I never saw him alive again.*

*He hunted-up Bruiser in town and it escalated from a bloody brawl to guns. Willard was shot and killed and they said it was 'tolerably' fair, whatever that meant. Bruiser got away with it, anyhow.*

*The Old Man got it out of me, through my sobbing over losing Willard – he was a mighty fine brother. Naturally, the Old Man blamed me for Willard's death.*

*After that was when he started beating me at any excuse, making some up if he couldn't find one.*

*'You piss-ant little swine! You gone and got my boy killed! Your own brother! Well, I ain't gonna let you forget tnat for the rest or your miserable life – and I promise you, I'll make it as miserable as I can.'*

*After a couple or months I ran away . . . and went to war.*

Once Bruiser knew I'd recognized him, he made no effort to hide his true identity.

'How come a Johnny Reb like you finished up as a Yankee colonel running your home town – and no one recognized you?' I asked him, though few would've seen through those scars. But I'd seen those sadistic eyes close-up; not something you forget.

His eyes were lashless now, watery and though appearing blank, the old hostility burned in their depths. He wheezed and coughed. Cookie persisted in ignoring him and the other man so neither had had any treatment yet. I ripped up some rags, soaked them in water and covered Bruiser's chest wound, tied one around the hip as well as I could, staunching the blood flow in part.

'Couple figured out who I was,' he said eventually, chest heaving. 'But I was in a position to get rid of 'em . . . and square away a lot more with them snooty sonuvers.'

'How'd you survive that Yankee shell? Seven others

with you were killed, blown to bits.'

The lipless slash of a mouth moved: it may have been an attempt at a half-smile. 'I was flung behind a sand ridge – clothes blown off. Not a stitch on me. Before the shell hit, I was draggin' a wounded Yankee officer along by his name tags slung round his neck on a thong – we'd captured him earlier – when they found me my face was like raw beefsteak. I must've still had the tags in my hand. So they figured I was Colonel Lawton like the tags said an' ... an' give me their best medical treatment. I weren't about to complain. But I was kind of scared when I started to come round in a Yankee hospital camp – played possum, listened to what they was sayin' 'bout this Lawton – finally figured out it was *me* they was talkin' about ... so I let 'em think that.'

He was exhausted but he didn't need to continue. The rest was easy to figure. He played Lawton, his face mutilated so no one recognized him. If he didn't know someone he was supposed to, as Lawton, all he had to do was blame it on the explosion: memory black-out. War ended, he needed a soft job, got one as adminstrator and eventually ended up in Amarillo – where the old Henry Bruiser Dexter showed through and he started settling old scores in the name of Reconstruction.

Somehow it back-fired, he was set down to be court-martialled, deserted – and now here he was.

'Your idea, that damned town?' I asked, and he nodded after a while, those eyes still burning way back with the old hatred for anyone named McQuade. I nodded suddenly. 'Skip in town would get word to you when a herd was coming north from Amarillo, eh? And you sent out your whores to soften-up the trail crew, then jumped 'em, killed 'em, sold the herd. You can change your name all you want, Bruiser, but you're still a Dexter low-life at the bottom of the barrel with all the other crawling maggots.'

His eyes flared and he mouthed a harsh curse. It was followed by blood and I bellowed for Cookie, *made* him come across. 'Tend him, Cookie! For God's sake, the man's dying!'

'You see Monte an' Latigo?' he countered grimly. 'They already dead! Thanks to this sonuver!'

'See what you can do,' I told him curtly and he went to work. I stood by, and I have to admit he did a pretty good job, but it was too late.

Bruiser Dexter died about an hour later. He called for me just before he went, one hand reaching feebly for my shirt sleeve. His eyes were glazing but that slash of a mouth stretched out – was it meant to be a smile, or some show of triumph? – and he said a few words, harsh, gurgling, almost unintelligible.

He'd been dead maybe ten minutes before I finally unscrambled those words. He'd said, each punctuated by painful dragging wheezes: '*Not – just – Skip – watchin' out. . . .*'

What the hell? The man was dying and yet he sounded almost – amused! And I didn't know what he meant.

Which was too bad. If I'd been able to work it out then, I just might have been able to save a few more lives.

Just maybe.

*

I was mighty glad to see the Raton Pass far behind us and our dust cloud lifting between the rear of the herd and far-off Pueblo.

It hadn't been easy getting the herd together again. At first it seemed like it would be just a hard day's work, but they had scattered up little brush-choked draws, hid themselves in poky dry washes and arroyos a man didn't even know were there until he sweated a gallon before noon and another one at least by sundown and even then had to stumble upon them.

Horses lost shoes, others were cracked or the nails worked loose and more time was lost replacing them. Lucky our blacksmith, 'Jacko' Jackson, who doubled as a point rider, had survived the raids and stampedes and had somehow managed to save all his tools.

But, finally, we meshed the various bunches of cows into a single herd and set off once more for points north.

We were edgy, red-eyed, hungry and thirsty – and more than ready for trouble. Some luckless Indian on a distant ridge, sitting his pony, minding his own business, but watching us as we rolled north, was blown to the Happy Hunting Grounds by a .58 calibre ball from Clegg's muzzle-loading '62 Murray rifle, a trophy he'd picked up for his father in distant Pennsylvania during the war. It had a built-in Vernier scale with peep-sight and the poor old redskin didn't stand a chance. He hadn't meant us any harm.

Tough on him, but it was an indication of our mood: none of us was prepared to take a chance, long shot – pardon the pun! – though it may be.

The days rolled by, hot, thirsty, dusty. We had grit everywhere, between our teeth, up our nostrils, in our eyes and just about any bodily orifice you care to name. Water was short and the trail was long.

Then one blazing morning – we weren't even in sight of Pueblo or the rail tracks, though I figured we must be getting close by now – a band of a dozen close-packed riders came over a grassy hill in a tight bunch. I groaned.

'Hell almighty! Almost there and some son of a bitch has saved his run at our herd till now!' I unslung the Henry, seeing the crew also reaching for their guns. Ammo was low so we'd have to make every bullet count. 'Shoot straight, boys!'

'Hold up, Stretch!' Clegg called suddenly, standing in the stirrups. 'Someone's calling out!'

Likely telling us to haul rein and stop the herd or they'd ride clear over us and shoot us as we went down under their hoofs. 'You hear that?' Toohey yelled.

'Hear what?' I snapped, angry that I hadn't deciphered the words as quickly as he'd done.

'He's from the Denver Meat Company and he bags first offer on our herd!' Toohey threw his dusty, battered hat into the air and cut loose with a rebel yell that almost started another stampede. 'Hear that, boys? We're gonna be rich!'

'I ain't!' yelled back Jacko. 'First gal Ah sees can help me spend my pay! Every damn cent of it!'

The others chorused and I grinned through the dirt as the new riders came in waving hats and cat-calling.

'If you like, we'll take over, friend,' a man in a dusty pin-striped suit called in my direction, doffing his hat and blotting sweat with the sleeve of his coat. 'You and your crew just take her easy now – we'll take the cows into town. Then we'll get to dickerin' price. You're the first herd got through in months and folk're beef-hungry.'

I felt the unravelling of a knot that had been just below my ribs since we'd popped the first longhorn out of the brush down on the Caprock. *We'd made it!*

The meat-agent added, 'I'm a fair man, Texan. I'll pay you top dollar.' He held out a hand. 'Shake on it?'

*Amen to that!*

# CHAPTER 13

# BACK TO TEXAS

To this day, my memories of Pueblo are mighty hazy.

At least I knew we'd lifted the lid off a town of that name: some of the crew didn't know – nor care – where the hell they'd been. But when our stay was over, we all had the shakes and our knees were weak and our pockets mostly empty – even though many of the friendly folk of Pueblo wouldn't let us pay for hardly anything. But, of course, there were shysters and greedy hangers-on, and the saloon gals who had to make a living: a few used one hand to caress some hot-breathing cowpoke while the other was exploring the pockets of his trousers on the chair beside the bouncing bed.

But that was what a trail town was all about so there were no real complaints, even from those nursing cuts and bruises after brawls.

The meat agent had been a fair dealer and we sold

all the cows – with a blanket price of $38.50 a head. No complaints from any of the ranchers who had joined our herd. We'd all lost steers along the way but that had to be accepted. Flag ended up with 1,465 head. So I had a nice bundle of dollars to hand the Old Man when I got back: see if that would make him happy!

Even deducting the head tax and trail expenses, there'd be plenty left to redevelop Flag and build it up into something like the big, prosperous spread it used to be. It would take years of work but that was OK – a man had to accomplish something he could be proud of in the time he lived.

I was looking forward to seeing Old Hiram's face. . . .

We rode together on the trail south and after a day or two had mostly shaken our Pueblo hang-overs. Then the urge to get back to familar territory in the Panhandle strengthened. We had sold our remuda, keeping out two horses apiece for the long ride back to Texas, so we covered distance at a good pace.

We rode through Raton Pass and across the Cimarron Cut-off, south of Capulin Mountain, before we ran into trouble. *Real* trouble, too.

There was a gap in a low line of hills, more a cutting than a pass, and Jacko was in the lead, asleep in the saddle, rolling with the easy movement of his horse and no doubt snoring. I was towards the rear with Clegg and Toohey, sometimes talking, other times all of us joining in on some range ditty a rider felt like singing. Blackie Lee, part Chinese, got his harmonica going now and again. He had used it to good purpose during the edgy night stops with the herd on the trail north, calming the cattle with soothing melodies.

He was working through some plaintive Irish tune as we headed into the cutting. Toohey started to sing, stumbling over the lyrics, having forgotten most of the words, when there was an echoing rifle blast and Jacko rolled backwards over his horse which took off with a sideways lunge before running, mane flying free, through the cutting.

We all started to haul rein – I say 'started' to because the volley of gunfire that followed that first shot came so damn fast the echoes of the bushwhacker's gun hadn't even begun to die away.

Someone to my left grunted and spilled from the saddle. I swore, crouched low, raking with spurs, slapping with rein ends, recognizing Toohey rolling through the dust. Clegg jumped his mount over the skidding body, unsheathed his carbine from the army scabbard on his McLellan saddle and threw it to his shoulder. His hat spun from his head and he swayed, almost falling.

I had no time to notice anything else. Lead fanned my face, actually clipped the lobe of my left ear, and I felt a warm spurt against my dirt-scaled neck as blood ran into the grubby collar of my shirt. Instinctively, I slid my left boot clear of stirrup, slipped my right hip down, swung my left leg over and clung to the horn one-handed, the claybank's stretching body between me and the wall where the shots had come from. More lead buzzed and whined. Dust spurts kicked up around the clay-bank's hoofs. My Henry was too long in the barrel to shoot from this position so I opened up with the Colt. The range was too far and with the violent motion of the racing horse I had little hope of hitting any of the enemy – whoever they were. They must be some more of the survivors of Heaven's Gateway, but 'who' didn't really matter right now. Killing the sons of bitches before they killed us was the priority.

I felt the slug take the claybank in the body, side of the chest, I figured. It swerved, a gusting breath exploding from it. Its head shook wildly, bewildered, and the front legs folded. I let go instantly, hit hard, snatching the Henry from the rope loop as I dropped. The Colt spun from my grip and then the earth smashed at my body and I lost breath and hide and my hat – but I kept a death-grip on the Henry. Maybe that was the wrong way to put it – *death grip.* . . .

There were lights and crazy glimpses of the rock walls, spurting smoke from the various places the ambushers were holed-up, charging horses with wild-eyed men crouching in their saddles, shooting pistols or carbines. I came abruptly to a sudden stop, hit a rock, felt like I'd broken every bone in my body, followed by a blinding sheet of light that disinte-grated into a thousand swirling stars.

Then I was still and, hurt and breathless though I was, the old instinct took over and somehow I crawled behind a low line of rocks. Chips stung my ear and neck, ricochets snarled: someone had

146

already found my cover.

Boot heels thrashing, I thrust my aching body, on my back, deeper amongst the rocks and got behind a large basalt boulder shaped like a shark's fin for protection. It was a good place: it leaned a little inwards, giving me some cover overhead, and the curve of the fin allowed me to shoot at the wall without exposing much of my body.

I wasted no time in raking the wall. A man jumped up startled, began to run for better cover. He never made it. A second man grabbed at the rifle the first one had dropped – likely for its ammo – and my next bullet shattered his arm at the elbow. He screamed, reared up involuntarily, and I shot him in the neck. Without waiting to see his rag-doll body fall, I swung the rifle's muzzle along the wall, found a third target, but this one was mighty fast, dropped out of sight, just a blur, even as I triggered.

But I'd gotten an impression of him: it might've been only for a twentieth of a second, but I damn well recognized the son of a bitch – Skip Dexter!

No time to think of the whys and wherefores, although it ran through my head instantly that he was after us for killing Bruiser – and after the money for the cattle now. Neither he nor Bruiser had had any success taking the herd from us, and, finally he had gotten smart enough to realize he should let us reach Pueblo, make the sale, *then* pick us off on the way south, while we were carrying the money.

Well, maybe I was just a mite smarter than Skip.

No more doubts about his identity as he bellowed,

'This is as close to Texas as you get, McQuade! Hope you're ready to die, you son of a bitch!'

For answer I emptied my magazine at the place I'd seen him drop out of sight and while the wasted lead whined away into the afternoon, I thumbed fresh rimfire cartridges out of my belt loops. Fourteen in the tube, one more in the breech – and I was ready for Skip and anything he cared to throw my way.

Toohey was still trying to get under cover. All this had happened in seconds and he had now regained enough breath from his fall to start hunting cover. Skip never gave him a chance. His rifle muzzle poked between two boulders and he put four shots into Toohey, my old pard's lean body twisting and jerking as the lead slammed home. *Cold-blooded bastard!*

'Who's next, McQuade?' Skip taunted. 'None of you is gonna get outta here! Just a matter of time while we pick you off one by one!'

Adam Clegg suddenly appeared, rising from behind a sandstone ridge, leaping on to the top, running along with his Army Remington slanted down. He fired into the place where Skip had been hiding – but two more guns hammered, one from above him, one from his right. He spun and slipped, jack-knifing over the ridge, losing his pistol. It didn't matter, because he slid back slowly out of sight, limp and bloody.

'You countin', Stretch?' Skip called, laughing.

I slid back. The other trail men had grouped now, their weapons mostly single-shot, and they were slow to reload against the repeaters Skip's men were using.

'Anyone see how many there are?' I called softly.

Red Kimborough, white-faced, blood on one arm, looked up. 'Only 'bout three, mebbe four, Stretch, but they got Spencers or Henrys like you!'

'Get loaded, all of you!' I said grimly.

'We're about there,' Red said. 'Say when!'

'Counting me, there're six of us. Red, take two to your left, stay low, keep working left. You'll come to at least two of the sonuvers. Don't let them get away. Rest of you come with me.'

I led them up the slope and Skip and his men picked away at us, but there were so many rocks studding the grade they couldn't get a clear shot. Then there was a racket of gunfire and shouting from below and Skip and his two sidekicks were distracted at the unexpected attack.

'Now!' I yelled to the men with me and threw myself between two low rocks, Henry firing, raking the boulders where the killers were partly exposed.

The trail hands triggered their single-shots and one of Skip's men collected a ball through the middle of the face. The second one jumped up as I fired at Skip and took the bullet I'd meant for Dexter, his head jerking violently.

And now I'd lost sight of Skip.

He hadn't waited to shoot it out with me, not without his men. He had no guts for a square-off. . . .

I started to leap from rock to rock, looking for him, fell sprawling, ripping my shin painfully. By the time I'd gotten back to my feet I heard a horse running at speed.

Lifting up, I saw Dexter whipping his buckskin out of the cutting and heading south, his red dust glowing in the sun, enveloping him. . . . I couldn't get a clear shot.

I swore and limped back to where Clegg and the others were waiting. Toohey was dead. So was Jacko. Two more men were hit and Adam Clegg was wounded in the left side, had a scalp-burn, and his ribs were hurt from his fall.

I looked at them grimly. 'Boys, you'll have to look after yourselves. Dexter's getting away, but I aim to finish this thing now. I'll take the two best horses and a canteen. Doctor each other and you'll make it back to Amarillo OK.'

Clegg nodded slowly, in great pain. 'Finish it, Stretch. What is it you fellers say? *Adios?*'

'More like *hasta la vista*. But we'll make a Texan out of you yet, Adam. Good luck, boys.'

By God, it was a long, long trail!

What made it that way was that Skip knew this country better than I did and that told me this wasn't the first time he and Bruiser and their pards had pulled this kind of deal.

Skip, hanging around Amarillo, was in a perfect position to know when the herds were coming up the Goodnight-Loving trail or making their own way north. It didn't necessarily have to be to the railheads in Colorado. Those wanting to head for Kansas or Missouri would still travel through Amarillo and part of the way we had followed.

Bruiser and his crew would be waiting once Skip had gotten word to them. Building the town, Heaven's Gateway, was a refinement now that the Goodnight-Loving trail was becoming known. But things had gone wrong when we had destroyed the town and they had had to resort to open attack on the herd. When that failed, someone got the notion of waiting until we were on the way back, after selling the steers, bringing the sale money with us.

Well, Skip never was too smart – plenty cunning, sure, but not really *smart*. Then. . . .

*Damn!* The son of a bitch got me! Just as I hit a twisted trail running alongside a low mesa, the tracks kind of jumbled, deliberately, I figured too late. While I slowed to sort them out, Dexter lay atop the rim and took his shot.

The bullet knocked me out of the saddle. It burned across the top of my left shoulder so I guess he was aiming for a headshot. Stupid move, Skip! Body shots are more reliable: if he'd spent time in the army he'd have known that. But his bullet put me down on the ground. Luckily I'd been riding holding the Henry in one hand. So I hit and rolled on to my belly, levered in a shell and gave him a faceful of rock chips from the edge of the rim with a lucky shot.

I saw him rear back and could imagine his curse at not having nailed me squarely. As I levered, he stayed out of sight and called down, 'I got plenty of time, Stretch! Still a long ways back to Flag. You ain't never gonna see it again, so make up your mind to that!'

151

I didn't waste breath answering, squirmed into as much cover as I could. Then the bastard shot my sorrel, leaving me the roan which wasn't as strong, although faster over short distances. The sorrel went down kicking and Dexter's laugh reached me above its dying squeals. There was a lot of blood seeping down my left arm and it made my hand slippery. But I lunged for the roan's trailing reins, caught them, and dragged it in tight against the broken rock wall as two fast shots kicked dust where it had been standing.

'Damn you, McQuade! You always did have the luck of the Irish!'

'Whatever luck you had just ran out, Skip! You ain't gonna see another sunrise!'

He yelled curses and emptied his rifle at me. I had to duck, cover my eyes against rockdust and chips. I coughed, spat, and heard his horse going away from the mesa. I hit the stirrup but fumbled and fell back. The roan was skittish and rolling its eyes, but I gentled it enough to mount and then I made myself wait while I reloaded the long magazine. I only had nine shells.

I wadded a kerchief under my torn shirt over the bleeding wound. Then I followed Dexter's dust trail as he weaved and dodged through the country ahead.

I almost got him in a gulch just over the New Mexico-Texas line. I figured out his line of travel and as this was back in country I knew now, I worked around and ahead and was waiting as he rode into the gulch. But I was too eager, or I'd lost so much blood that my hands shook. My bullet put a brand across his face and I swore – I, too, had made the mistake of taking a headshot on a moving target instead of a body one! *Blamed fool!*

I couldn't afford to waste ammunition. I checked the the Colt I'd recovered before I left Clegg and the others. Three chambers loaded – they would have to do. Wearily I mounted and kept my distance. I knew where he was headed now, knew the best places for ambush and avoided them. To check my hunch I climbed a ridge – it *hurt* using my left arm – and had the satisfaction of seeing Dexter taking the trail south. I followed for two more days and figured to close with him in Amarillo around sundown or a mite later on the second day.

I was wrong. At the junction of the trails, instead of heading into Amarillo, he took the fork that led to Flag!

Swearing, I raked with my spurs but I knew the roan could never catch him before he reached the ranch.

There were little-known trails vaguely remembered from my boyhood that would allow me to get there almost on his heels, but could I find them again. . . ?

I did, but he beat me to Flag by at least an hour.

I came in on foot, using the corral and barn for cover, Henry cocked and ready for bear, Colt loose in my holster. There was a body sprawled by the garden – I felt sick as I recognized poor young Denny. He seemed to be still alive, moving slightly, some blood showing in his sandy hair. A deadly cold fury spread over me as I went looking for Skip. I found him on the front porch with the Old Man, the Chapman woman and, of all people, Kitty Byron.

He was holding her by one arm and she was pale and frightened, but still with a determined set to her mouth. The Old Man sat huddled in his wheel-chair, the blackthorn walking stick in the loop I'd set up so he could reach it easily. His face was gaunt, sunken more than I recollected. But the set of his mouth told me he was stewing like a cauldron inside, the old, rheumatic-mangled hands opening and closing as far as they were able. His eyes never left Skip.

Ellie Chapman sat in a shaded area in a rattan chair, calmly fanning herself with a Spanish fan that I recognized as once having belonged to my mother.

'Come on in, Stretch!' Skip called suddenly, making me start. 'You can see who I've got here. Bit of luck. She came visitin' old Hiram to see if he'd had any news about you. Was gettin' ready to leave just as I arrived. Reckon I haven't run outa luck yet, like you said, you son of a bitch! So you just come in empty-handed – except for the money you got for the cows! You can bring that!'

I couldn't get a clear shot at him without endangering Kitty. If I moved left, I'd have a shot, but the Old Man was too close then. So I eased down the Henry's hammer, laid it on the ground, and stepped out, hands at shoulder level. The Colt sagged some in my old holster.

'Wrong about your luck, Skip,' I said, and he

quickly brought Kitty around in front of him. 'You shouldn't've shot Denny. I won't let you get away with that – and I don't have any money with me.'

Peripherally, I saw the Old Man stiffen and the Chapman woman's fan stopped as her eyes narrowed and she sat up straighter, more stiffly. Kitty looked at me pleadingly and Dexter tightened his grip, making her wince.

'You always did have a queer sense of humour! You better be joshin' right now!'

I shook my head. 'Too much money to carry all those back trails south with coyotes like you waiting along 'em,' I told Dexter, and I saw that he knew I was speaking gospel. 'Why, there was most of fifty thousand bucks – don't that make your mouth water, Skip?'

He bared his yellow teeth, shook Kitty and brought a cry of pain from her. I tensed and he pulled her right across his body. 'Don't try nothin', Stretch! She don't have to die right off, you know.' His gun barrel moved down her body and pressed in her skirts around the back of her thigh. 'See? Fifty thousand! Better'n we expected, but it don't make up for you killin' Bruiser!'

Ellie lifted out of her chair, face white. 'Hank's dead?'

*Hank!* What a damn fool I was! Hank was a nickname for Henry – Bruiser's real name – and she had told me once, that Hank would soon pull me into line! *So what the hell was this?* Bruiser Dexter and Eleanor Chapman? '*Not just Skip watchin' out,*' Bruiser had said. . . .

No time to try to figure it out. Skip asked, 'Where's the money, damn you?'

'In the Amarillo bank. I had the meat agent send a bank draft on ahead by mail for deposit into Flag's account. It's where you can't reach it, Skip.'

I think that even impressed the Old Man – briefly.

'You damn fool!' That was Ellie Chapman, shaking with fury, small fists clenched, the fan crushed to splinters in one hand as she glared at Skip.

'Aw, shut up!' Dexter snarled. 'I've had enough takin' orders from you!'

She scoffed, 'If I hadn't told you what to do, you'd've been lynched long ago, you idiot! You and your stupid brother.'

'Stupid? Bruiser? You was gonna marry him – that'd make you stupid, too, wouldn't it?'

She saw my puzzled face and smiled crookedly. 'It's simple, Dean. My real name is Eleanor Lawton. Colonel Lawton was my husband. When he was supposedly badly scarred in an explosion, the army allowed me to visit him – or the man who claimed to be him.'

'Bruiser! Hank?'

She nodded. 'Of course I knew he wasn't my husband and I got the truth out of him. I was kind of attracted to him somehow – all those scars – and in the course of a few visits he told me his life story. I was working for the Reconstruction at the time and suddenly I saw a way of getting my hands on a big property that would give me security for life – Flag.'

'Using Bruiser, posing as Colonel Lawton, in charge of Reconstruction here, to bankrupt Hiram and leave the way open for you to walk in and take over,' I said, getting ahead of the bitch.

She didn't like it and her face was murderous.

'Yes! But the fool couldn't pass up the chance to settle old scores with enemies he'd made in Amarillo over the years. He went too far and deserted. But I saw how I could still worm my way into this old fool's favours.' She gestured at the silent Hiram. 'Skip fixed his saddle so he'd break his legs, and I was on hand, full of sympathy, nurse and companion-adviser – wasn't I, Hiram, dear?'

He snorted and probably only I recognized the urge to kill flaring in those old eyes.

'And Bruiser was still hanging around up the trail,' I said, 'all fired up with the Dexters' well-known greed. Then I returned with the notion of driving a big herd north to market where meat prices were sky-high and . . .'

I didn't have to go on: it was self-evident and she made no attempt to deny anything. But all their attention was on me now. And it shouldn't have been. . . .

The Old Man reached up, yanked the steel-hard blackthorn walking stick from its wall sling and flung it at Skip. Dexter must have heard the faint *whoosh!* as the stick flailed towards him, spun, trying to yank Kitty around, too. She thrust a leg between his and he stumbled and she broke free as the stick whacked him on the head.

Ellie was reaching for a rifle propped against the wall and Kitty flung herself upon her and that was all I saw.

157

Skip regained balance, twisted towards me with a savage snarl, bringing up his gun. But mine was already free of leather and the pistols roared as one – except my Colt roared again, and once more with my last bullet.

Skip's lead gouged a large splinter out of the rail. All my three bullets slammed into his heavy body driving him backwards. His hips hit the rail, splintering it. He crashed into the yard, sprawled there on his back, arms spread like a crucifix, shirtfront bloody.

Someone screamed and I whirled in time to see Kitty drive Ellie Chapman face-first into the wall beside the door. Ellie fell to her knees, sobbing, nose bleeding. Kitty gave me a tremulous smile and I held out my hand. She took it and squeezed tightly as she came in against me, clinging to my wounded arm. 'I – I've never done anything like that before!'

'You did good, Kit,' I told her, and looked at the Old Man, while she went to examine the stirring Denny. 'You can still come good when needed, Pa.'

His old eyes locked with mine. '*You* were the one damn well needed me!'

'I'm glad you stepped in – I told you I'd come back to help you get Flag up and running again.'

'Well, I always taught you to be a man of your word.' He snorted. 'Now, show me you learned the lesson good! There's another canyon you dunno about: must be five, six hundred longhorns in there by now. . . .'

My jaw dropped. 'Hell! I just got back!'

'There's work to be done, dammit, lotsa work. Oh,

an' by the way, in that old chest in my room, wrapped in oilskin, there's a pair of saddle-bags I had made by old Sebastiano. They was for your fifteenth birthday, but you damn well run off and went to war, ungrateful whelp! Still ain't sure you deserve them fine bags!'

Just like him: give and take away, all in the blink of an eye. Kitty came back just then, smiling. 'Denny's only got a scalp crease: he'll be all right.' She turned to Pa.

'Surely Dean has proved to you he's earned the right to those saddle-bags by now, Mr McQuade. He deserves them – and your respect after all he's done for Flag.'

It was a strange feeling, having a small beautiful woman like Kitty standing up for me. Strange, but something I could get used to gladly.

The Old Man glared at her. 'This ain't your business, miss, but I guess you see it as standin' by your man. . . .'

When Kitty smiled up at me, I felt a tightness in my chest, a pleasant tightness, and she held my arm more firmly. Hiram McQuade snorted once again, looking directly at me now.

'Gimme that stick so's I can get outa this goddamn chair! Time I took an interest in seein' how you're runnin' this place.' He glanced at the sprawled, sobbing Ellie Chapman. 'Too many people been tellin' me what to do for too long.'

'It's your ranch, Pa: you're in charge.'

'I damn well better be!'

I helped him to his feet and he leaned shakily on the blackthorn stick. He said curtly, 'Reckon you can use them saddle-bags. But you damn well gotta earn my respect yet!'

Well, *I guess he'd never change. But maybe I wouldn't want him to.* After all, it *was* my fault Willard had got killed: I still had a penance to do there, and I knew he was telling me that. Then it hit me:

*Rebuild Flag as a memorial to Willard.*

Even the Old Man couldn't bitch about that.

'Sounds like an OK deal to me, Pa,' I told him.

Pw